She had to warn them. 'The car. You mustn't drive the car. There's going to be an accident.'

The woman's hiss of surprise was almost drowned out by the man's hoot of laughter. 'You do believe in giving your customers their money's worth, don't you? For a moment there I thought you were having a fit. But, as I say, save it for someone who'll appreciate it. This nonsense is beginning to irritate me.' He pushed back the chair and stood up to leave.

'Please!' Her voice was stronger now. 'Please, I'm not joking, I saw it. You mustn't drive the car.'

'Don't be ridiculous. Come on Mandy—we're leaving.'

But the woman hung back. 'No, Dirk, wait. Maybe we ought to listen to her. She means it. She's not acting. Couldn't we leave the car here?'

'What? And walk all the way back to the village? You must be mad. Just get it through your superstitious little head that she's just trying it on.' He swung back to Sasha. 'What's the going rate for a genuine gypsy's warning then? Or is it all part of the service?'

LOVE'S DESTINY

BY

ELEANOR REES

MILLS & BOON LIMITED
ETON HOUSE   18-24 PARADISE ROAD
RICHMOND   SURREY   TW9 1SR

*First published in Great Britain 1989
by Mills & Boon Limited*

© Eleanor Rees 1989

*Australian copyright 1989
Philippine copyright 1989
This edition 1989*

ISBN 0 263 76413 3

*Set in Times Roman 11 on 12¼ pt.
01-8909-48549 C*

Made and printed in Great Britain

CHAPTER ONE

SASHA could feel the derision in the stranger's dark eyes prickling the back of her neck as she caressed each broad finger in turn, stroking from base to tip with practised delicacy. It was a good, strong hand; hard-muscled under the warm skin. A very masculine hand: stubborn, down-to-earth and practical, with little use for tact or diplomacy.

Well, she hadn't needed the solid thumbs to tell her that. Dragged into the tent by his blonde companion, their owner had made no secret of his scepticism. She felt the pads which in more violent days would have held the hilt of a sword; they were high and firm. The hand of a leader, then; of a man who would know exactly what he wanted and would be prepared to reach out and take it. It—or her; it was a lover's hand, too, full and sensual in its strength. Sasha shivered, her mind momentarily invaded by the image of its roughness against soft female skin. Her skin. Pushing the thought away, she looked up and met his eyes.

And then it happened. Something seemed to explode inside her head, catapulting her into another, horrific reality. A world of noise and fire, as tyres screeched and metal ripped like cloth about her. The dark, angular face opposite was veiled in flame, twisting and distorting as the flickering tongues licked higher. Sasha opened her mouth to scream, but the heat seared her lungs and no sound came.

'What the devil?' She felt the hand jerked roughly from her grasp and slowly the world began to swim back into focus. 'What the hell do you think you're doing? Save the amateur dramatics for someone who'll be impressed.'

'No!' Another voice now; a woman. Sasha felt weak and drained, as if she had given blood. The voices seemed to be a long way off. 'Can't you see she's not pretending?' Then softer and closer. 'Are you ill? Can I get you anything?'

'I'll be all right.' Sasha hardly recognised her own voice. 'Perhaps some water. On the side table.' A wet glass was thrust into her hand and she sipped it gratefully. 'It was so clear...'

'What was?' It was the woman again. Sasha tried to focus, but the long blonde hair and lovely features which she had noticed when the pair came in seemed to waver before her eyes.

She had to warn them. 'The car. You mustn't drive the car. There's going to be an accident.'

The woman's hiss of surprise was almost drowned out by the man's hoot of laughter. 'You do believe in giving your customers their money's worth, don't you? For a moment there, I thought you were having a fit. But, as I say, save it for someone who'll appreciate it. This nonsense is beginning to irritate me.' He pushed back the chair and stood up to leave.

'Please!' Her voice was stronger now. 'Please, I'm not joking. I saw it. You mustn't drive the car.'

'Don't be ridiculous. Come on, Mandy—we're leaving.'

But the woman hung back. 'No, Dirk, wait. Maybe we ought to listen to her. She means it. She's not acting. Couldn't we leave the car here?'

'What? And walk all the way back to the village? You must be mad. Just get it through your superstitious little head that she's simply trying it on.' He swung back to Sasha. 'What's the going rate for a genuine gypsy's warning, then? Or is it all part of the service?'

'No...' She tried desperately to marshal her thoughts. What could she say to convince him? 'The car...' Remembering was agonisingly difficult, the memories slipping away like smoke. 'It was big; big and light-coloured, I think...'

'Yes!' The woman broke in eagerly. 'A white Range Rover. Dirk, you see; she does know what she's saying.'

'I'm sure she does.' His initial anger seemed to have been overtaken by a dry amusement. 'And you're exactly the sort of mug these people pray for. She didn't tell you about the car, you little idiot; you told her. And no doubt if you'd been here alone, you'd have told her your entire life history and come out convinced she read it in her crystal ball.'

'But——'

'No buts. If you think I'm walking a mile and a half in the rain just to satisfy your sense of romance, you can think again. The only reason I let you drag me in here in the first place was because it looked reasonably dry. Now stop fussing, will you? We have to be back at the hotel in half an hour, and I want another scout round first.'

Without waiting for an answer, he turned and walked swiftly out of the tent, flicking back the door-flap impatiently. After a moment's hesitation, the woman followed him. Sasha stared helplessly after them. Never in her life had she had such a clear premonition, or such a bleakly explicit one. Somehow, she had to stop them. But how?

Her young cousin shook his head stubbornly, although she had seen a gleam of interest at her suggestion. 'No, Sasha, I can't risk it. I'm on probation, remember? It'ud be cutting me own throat.'

Her heart sank. She had forgotten about that. The fifteen-year-old's passion for cars had landed him in court, on a charge of joy-riding. But the couple would be back soon; half an hour the man— Dirk, was that what she had called him? Somehow it rang a vague bell—had said. She had to try.

'Please, Tom,' she coaxed. 'I'd do it if I could, but I couldn't even get into it. And I'll take the blame. Gran would want us to do something.' She saw him hesitate and pressed home her advantage. 'I was standing in for her when it happened, Tom. She'd want you to do it. Only you must hurry. They'll be back in about ten minutes.'

'Ten minutes? I could get into that in ten seconds.' His tone of contempt reassured her. He was going to do it. 'But you tell'un it were you, OK? I don't want police come poking around.'

'Yes, yes, I'll tell them. Only hurry!'

She watched in fevered impatience as he pulled something from his pocket and fiddled covertly with the lock of the big white car. The door swung open almost as quickly as if he had had the key, and he was soon delving around under the open bonnet. Five minutes later, he pressed an oily lump of metal into Sasha's hand.

'There you go, then. It won't get far without that. But I weren't nothing to do with it, remember. I ain't been here.' And, turning his back, he slipped quickly into the bustle of the fair.

Sasha hitched up the heavy brocade folds of her unfamiliar costume and tucked the greasy object into the money-purse under her apron. Then, trying not to visualise the stranger's probable reaction to the news that she had disabled his car, she settled herself to await his return.

She wasn't left long in suspense. Almost as soon as her cousin was out of sight, she noticed a tall figure moving purposefully through the crowd towards the car park, the blonde head of his companion bobbing after him as she hurried to keep up. Sasha braced herself. Even without her grandmother's crystal ball, she could predict that this was going to be a stormy interview.

'You! You don't give up easily, do you?' His tone was light, but the underlying anger was still there. 'Look, Madame Zara, or whatever you call yourself, I appreciate the concern for my welfare. I'm even prepared to give you the benefit of the doubt and assume that you believe your own mumbo-jumbo. But you're frightening this lady and you're beginning to wear my patience very thin. So can we take the warning as read and get into the car? I have an appointment that I don't intend to miss.'

Sasha stood aside silently and let them pass. After all, it was no longer necessary to convince this pig-headed sceptic that she might just know what she was talking about. Like it or not, he was going to walk back to the village. And, given the choice, she thought she would probably prefer to make her confession with him safely imprisoned in the car.

It took him three or four turns of the key to re-alise that the car wasn't going to start, and at first it plainly didn't occur to him to connect the problem with Sasha's presence. It was almost comical to see his serious, furrowed expression as he tried to work out why the laws of nature, science and the internal combustion engine had temporarily been sus-pended. The girl was the first to guess at the con-nection. Her jaw dropped and she clambered out of the car to stare at Sasha in awe.

'You've put a spell on it!'

It was too much. Sasha burst out laughing, de-spite the fact that the man was now directing at her a look of pure ice. He waited expressionlessly until she had finished, and then the window which sep-arated them whirred down with a smoothness that could only be automatic.

'I'm glad you find the situation amusing. For your sake, I sincerely hope that this particular special effect was obtained without any permanent damage to my car. I don't know what you hope to gain by harassing me like this, but I can assure you that I won't hesitate to call in the police if it doesn't stop.'

The threat was delivered in the same precise, level tone as the rest of the speech; the effect was dry, almost pedantic. Like a lawyer speaking on behalf of a client. Only the dark glinting of his eyes betrayed the anger simmering under his calm shell, but Sasha was suddenly very glad that the car door stood between them.

'I'm sorry,' she started, then broke off. Why should she apologise to him? 'I've disabled it,' she stated bluntly. 'I took a—a bit out to make sure you couldn't drive it. It's not damaged, but I'm not going to give you back the missing part until I'm sure the danger is past.'

He tried to interrupt, but she raised her voice and pressed on. 'Look, I know you're angry, but try seeing it from my point of view, will you? You may think it's rubbish, but my family have had the Sight for generations. It doesn't happen often with me, and that was the clearest I've ever experienced, and I trust it. If I let you drive away and you were both killed, how do you think I would feel? I had to do something. It's not exactly far back to the village, if that's where you're staying. And the rain's easing off.'

Sasha stopped abruptly, suddenly aware that she was gabbling. What was it about him that made her feel so uneasy? He was staring at her now with a hostile mixture of astonishment and dawning suspicion.

'Just who—and what—are you?' he ground. 'You're no gypsy...and come to think of it, I think

I've seen you somewhere before. Is this some kind of elaborate joke? Because if so, I think it's gone far enough. Now, are you going to give me back whatever it is you've taken, or do I have to take steps to make you?'

The car door swung violently open and his long, jean-clad legs swung out on to the muddy ground. Sasha backed away uncertainly. She considered running, but realised immediately that she couldn't hope to outdistance him, hampered as she was by her elaborate costume. She would have to bluff it out.

'I haven't got it,' she said hurriedly. 'I've hidden it. You'll just have——'

A commotion in the lane outside the field interrupted them: a battered old truck narrowly making it through the gate, skidding wildly on the wet turf, and screeching to a stop about ten yards away. A man jumped out, and Sasha recognised one of the gypsy stall-holders, a distant relation of her grandmother's.

His face was whiter than his grubby shirt, and Sasha thought for a moment that he was going to vomit. He struggled to get the words out, but even before he spoke she knew with a kind of sick relief what his news was going to be.

'Down Pedlars Hill——' he gasped eventually. 'Get the 'ospital. It's Dan Smith; his brakes went in the lorry. His lads're there now, but they can't get him out. He's hurt bad, I think.'

'I'll phone them from here.' The stranger took command, as if the man had addressed him from the start, but Sasha bit back her resentful comment

when she saw him reach back inside the Range
Rover and pick up the handpiece of a carphone.
The nearest public box was on the far side of the
site; perhaps overbearing, bad-tempered, pig-
headed men with closed minds had their uses, after
all.

'There's an ambulance on its way,' he said a few
minutes later. 'What about his family?'

'They'll be told. We'll look after that. Thank you
for your help, sir.' It was unmistakably a rebuff.
The gypsy had recovered his composure, and with
it his reserve. The circle had been redrawn, and the
tall man was definitely on the outside.

Sasha felt a sneaking sense of satisfaction at his
discomfiture, even though she knew that she too
was excluded. Tolerated for her grandmother's
sake, she was out of place in the fair community
at a time like this. It was time to go. She watched
the gypsy out of sight and then turned back to the
couple by the Range Rover.

'You may as well have this.' She fished under her
apron and brought out the greasy engine part. 'Your
accident seems to have happened without you.'

Without waiting for the stranger's reaction, she
turned and walked away, suddenly weak and
tremulous with relief. Behind her, she could hear
voices raised in argument. One word came through
loud and clear, with all the power of masculine
lungs and prejudice behind it.

'Coincidence.'

The light inside the caravan was dim and restful
with the curtains drawn. Sasha slipped off the old-

fashioned costume and folded the heavy, embroi-
dered fabric with care. It felt almost indecent to be
wearing as little as the skirt and blouse revealed
beneath, although out of deference for her grandmother neither were skimpily cut. 'How old are
these things, Gran?'

'Older than me, some of them.' The old woman
sat proudly in her high-backed chair, her shrewd
black eyes bright with the pleasures of memory.
'The jacket's the oldest; that was my grandmother's making. And the apron's the newest; it
was your mother stitched that.'

She smiled reminiscently. 'And a right fuss she
made about it, too; never could bear to be doing
a thing for more than five minutes together. And
yet once your father learned her to read, she'd sit
for hours with her face in a book. Loving changes
people, right enough.' Then, abruptly, 'What about
this man, then, *kushti*?'

The sudden change of subject took Sasha off
balance. 'What do you mean?'

'What do you think, girl? What's he like, this
Gorgio who has you seeing visions in his palm and
getting your cousin in trouble? Do you know him?'

'Know him?' Sasha had expected to find that her
grandmother was well abreast of the afternoon's
events, but this suggestion surprised her. 'No, why
should I? He just came in when I was standing in
for you in the fortune-telling tent.' Or was dragged
in, she thought more accurately, remembering his
reluctance and the blonde girl's pleading. 'I've
never seen him before.'

'Only they say he works in the television as well.'

Sasha smiled, and shook her head. 'I don't know that many television people, Gran. It's a big field and I'm only really on the fringes of it. I don't even know his second name.'

But as she said it, her mind made the connection. 'Oh! Unless it's Dirk Kendrick—his girlfriend did call him Dirk, and it's an unusual enough name . . . If it is him, he's quite famous. He makes documentaries. But what would he be doing out here? His stuff is all inner-city squalor and urban crime and stuff like that.'

'Yes, Kendrick; that was the name.' It didn't occur to Sasha to wonder how her grandmother knew all this. The old woman's intelligence system would have been the envy of any major power. 'He's got a big van with cameras and the like down at the Feathers, and the word is he's wanting to film the fair.'

'Really? They won't like that, will they?' Sasha knew how reluctant the fair people were to be photographed, even informally and by those they trusted. The old superstitious fear had been reinforced by a more modern need to remain anonymous and untraceable in a world of hostile officialdom.

'I know nothing about it, Gran; but if you like, I can try and find out.' Now, why had she said that? The last thing she wanted was to come into any further contact with Mr Coincidence Kendrick. Wasn't it?

Her grandmother nodded, and Sasha suddenly noticed how worried she looked. Almost old. 'I'd be glad if you would, child. There's trouble brewing, I can smell it. There's been a run of bad luck this last summer; people are getting edgy. On top of Dan Smith's accident, this filming could be the spark to catch the tinder. Talk to him for me, *kushti*. With you being in the business, he might listen to you.'

'I'll try, Gran; I promise. But don't hold out too much hope; I don't think Mr Kendrick is in the habit of listening to other people's views.'

'You didn't like him, then?' The old voice was slyly questioning.

'No! At least...' Sasha realised with surprise that there was no easy answer to that question. 'He annoyed me, I suppose. He was so sure that he was right—and that sort of pig-headed arrogance drives me up the wall.'

'He didn't believe you?'

'Not only that—he was hostile, angry.'

'It's fear, *kushti*. People fear what they cannot understand; men most of all. Even the best of men.'

'I wouldn't have thought he was afraid of much. He's a very...uncompromising man, I would think. He'd make a bad enemy.' Sasha found she felt an obscure desire to be fair in her assessment. 'But I suppose if you needed him, if you were in trouble...' She remembered the calm way he had taken charge when news of the accident arrived; the impression of strength she had felt from his hand. 'Well, you'd be glad he was there.'

She felt her grandmother looking at her, and reddened without being very sure why. But the old woman made no direct comment. Instead, she gestured imperiously towards the mirrored dresser which contained her china and the other precious collectings of a lifetime's travelling. 'Put the kettle on, will you, girl? And bring the cards. I'll lay them out for you before you go.'

'Oh, no, Gran—don't.' Why did she feel so reluctant? Normally she found it fascinating to watch her grandmother interpreting the battered cards; as a child, it had been a rare treat. Only today, too much had already happened, and she wasn't sure that she could cope with any more.

But the old lady would have none of it. 'Don't be silly, girl. I'm entitled to a little curiosity at my age, surely? You can be shuffling them while the tea brews.'

Sasha knew when she was beaten. She put the kettle on to boil in the spotlessly clean little kitchenette, and obediently fetched the carved wooden card-box from the dresser.

'Got a question you want to ask the cards, *kushti*? Or just a general reading?'

'Oh, just general, Gran.' There were questions enough buzzing in her head, but at the moment she wasn't sure she wanted to put any of them into words, much less submit them to her grandmother's inquisitive mixture of intuition and intelligence. In her hands, the cards had an unnerving habit of hitting nails squarely on heads, and Sasha had never been sure how much was the real Romany gift, and how much the result of diligent information-gathering and a lifetime's experience of people.

Sasha watched as the old woman riffled expertly through the cards to pick out the one which would form the centre of the spread, representing Sasha herself. Then she passed the rest of the deck across the table. Sasha took them and let them run slowly through her fingers, feeling the age of them in their fuzzy edges and corners dog-eared with long use.

The act of shuffling had a calming effect, as always, taking her out of the bustle of the day's events to another, more peaceful, world. And, as she laid the cards back down on the lacy tablecloth, Sasha realised just how much of a strain the events of the afternoon had been.

At least here she could forget Kendrick and his arrogant treatment. Tomorrow she would go and see him, as her grandmother had asked, but for now he couldn't touch her. She reached over to pour the tea, while the old lady spread the cards into the traditional pattern.

But with the very first card turned over, she knew it had been a mistake. 'The King of Swords, *kushti*! Dark and handsome, was he, your Gorgio?'

'Not my Gorgio, Gran.' Why hadn't she refused the tea and left? 'Even if I wanted him, which I don't, he had a lady-friend with him this afternoon.' She had to admit that the angular face of the pasteboard king did bear more than a passing resemblance to her visitor—there was something about the way the eyes looked at you and through you, dark and piercingly intelligent...

'And reversed, too. There's going to be sparks there, my girl. And the ace right next door; that's a love-affair—a stormy one.'

'Look, Gran——' The walls of the little caravan seemed suddenly to press in on her. She might have guessed her grandmother wouldn't leave the subject alone. 'I don't——'

'And the Tower; that's trouble.' The note of glee died out as she looked at Sasha in concern. 'He's going to hurt you, *kushti*. And a journey over water——'

'Stop it!' Suddenly, it was all too much. Sasha jumped up, but her hand accidentally caught the lacy fringe of the tablecloth and jerked it, sending cards and tea-cups flying across the caravan. Broken china, cards and tea-leaves littered the floor. And from the midst of the destruction, the King of Swords stared up accusingly, its face the face of Dirk Kendrick.

Sasha stared at the wreckage, tears stinging her eyes. All the tension and frustration of the day seemed to come together in a flash-flood of emotion that tore away her defences like matchstick bridges. Blindly she felt for the door of the caravan and half fell down the steps into the damp fresh air. She had to get away.

CHAPTER TWO

Sasha didn't stop running until she reached the van, ignoring the curious stares of stall-holders and customers as she pushed her way through. Not until she dropped on to the tattered leather of the driving seat and felt the smooth coldness of the steering wheel under her hands did Sasha's heart-rate begin to slow.

The van was her haven. Even the scent of it reassured her: the familiar mixture of oil and old cooking smells encapsulating the memories of all the blissfully untrammelled holidays she had spent in its cramped accommodation. It was her passport to freedom; the last remnant of her wandering heritage. And somehow the knowledge that it was always there, its petrol tank full and the cupboards stocked, made the urge to escape more manageable.

Sasha breathed deeply, forcing herself to relax. She had behaved stupidly, of course. Looking back, she wasn't even sure what had upset her so much about the reading. She was familiar enough with the cards to know that the interpretation her grandmother had put on them was only one possibility; one chosen because it fitted in with the old lady's own preconceived ideas. If she had just laughed it off...

But now she would get no peace. Her panicky flight from the caravan would be all her grandmother needed to convince her that she was on the right track; there would be little chance of persuading her that Kendrick was the last type of man to interest her granddaughter.

The mere thought of the man was enough to make her temper start to rise. She took another deep breath and turned on the ignition, banishing him firmly from her mind.

At last the engine coughed into life and she headed back towards the village. As she slowed down for the corner on to Pedlars Hill, the wreckage of Dan Smith's lorry still lay embedded in the ditch—a sobering confirmation that, whatever happened, she had done the right thing.

Kendrick would never believe it, but she knew. If she hadn't intervened, his Range Rover would have been part of that twisted metal heap, and he and his girlfriend would have accompanied Dan to the hospital—or worse.

The thought was unexpectedly painful. On impulse, she cancelled the indicators, put her foot on the accelerator, and kept straight ahead. The old van did its best to respond. The road climbed steadily until at last she emerged from the tree-lined lane and could see the rolling Cotswold farmland spread out beneath her, its rich greens misted with rain.

Sasha felt for a few moments the tempting exhilaration of freedom. She didn't have to go back. She could just keep going and she would never have to see Dirk Kendrick again, never have to face her grandmother's scorn for her childish behaviour. The impulse was almost overwhelming...

But not quite. At the last minute, she swung the van round a corner into a lane which would bring her back into Horley by a different route. Not this time. But one day, she knew, she would take the road in earnest. And follow it all the way.

The bath water was hot, and Sasha had added a generous dose of her most extravagantly expensive bath oil. She lay back and let the clouds of scented steam soothe the last of the day's worries from her mind. What was there to worry about, after all? Tomorrow was a long way away. And she could cope with Kendrick. She felt almost sorry for him. He was in for something of a shock.

Until she had faced the bathroom mirror a few minutes before, it had completely slipped her mind that she was still wearing Madame Zara's heavy make-up. With her eyes darkly ringed with kohl, and her naturally pale skin powdered to a mystic pallor, she had to admit that she looked every bit the fairground fortune-teller. No wonder he had thought her warning was all part of the act; just a ruse to earn an extra tip.

But tomorrow she would meet him as Sasha Dinwoodie, freelance journalist and television presenter. This time, he wouldn't be able to patronise her. She would knock him dead.

Sleepily, she began to plan her campaign. There was the slinky red dress that she had worn for the programme on tea-leaves—but that was rather over the top for Horley, even to wow Dirk Kendrick. Against her dark colouring, the effect was dramatic, but it always made her feel that she needed a rose clenched between her teeth to complete the picture.

Or what about the electric blue catsuit from the one about reading head-bumps—what was it called? Phrenology, that was it. That had certainly gone down well with the director. He had made a determined effort to read her bumps after that session— only it hadn't been her head he was interested in.

Sasha smiled at the memory, sinking a little deeper into the cooling bath, luxuriating in the smooth touch of oil on her skin. She knew perfectly well that it was her striking appearance that had won her original chance on the programme. She had inherited her mother's gypsy flair for the dramatic—and the experience had taught her that clothes could be a weapon as well as a toy. But weapons had to be chosen with care. It was a difficult decision. And she was so sleepy...

Whether the water tickling her nose had woken her up to hear the doorbell, or whether the doorbell had just saved her from a highly scented, watery death, she wasn't quite sure. But the possibility that it might have been the latter quashed her irritation at being disturbed in the bath. She padded damply down the stairs, wrapping herself in a towel for decency.

Her hand was actually on the latch before it occurred to her to wonder who it might be—and in the same fraction of a second came the realisation that it might be Kendrick himself. He might even have come to apologise—but no, that was fantasy. More likely his car had been damaged in some way by Tom's attentions, and he had come to demand redress.

Sasha froze in position like a toy with the battery removed, her self-confidence suddenly evaporated. She didn't want to face him like this... But he would have heard her; he would know she was here. She had to answer the door.

It was a woman. Sasha felt relief wash over her as she pulled the door open—and then stepped back as she realised who the woman was. Dirk Kendrick's girlfriend was standing on the doorstep, looking cool and elegant—and very slightly embarrassed.

Sasha was the first to recover from a surprise that was obviously mutual. 'Oh! Hello, er...'

'Mandy,' supplied the other girl. Sasha noticed now that she was younger than she had seemed at first glance; probably no older than Sasha herself. 'Mandy Jenner. I was looking for someone called Sasha. Have I got the right address?'

'I'm Sasha.' The visitor's air of confusion puzzled her. Then it clicked. The girl didn't recognise her! 'Don't worry, you've got the right place. Come in.' She stood aside to let her past and closed the door behind her. 'Through to the left there. Sit down, will you, and I'll just go and put something on.'

When Sasha returned, her guest was sitting on the edge of the sofa, only the fidgeting of her hands with the clasp of her handbag betraying the fact that she wasn't as poised as she seemed. Sasha noted her nervousness with interest, as if they were back in the fortune-telling tent and she was looking for clues.

'Always make them wait; and watch them waiting,' her grandmother had told her in the stolen days of her childhood when she had skipped school to spend precious time at the fair. 'It's not just palms that tell stories. The more you know before you start, the more you'll see.'

'It was nice of you to come.'

The other girl jumped up and held out her hand. 'I'm sorry if I've disturbed you,' she said awkwardly, 'but I felt I had to talk to you—and thank you. You are Madame Zara, aren't you? I didn't know you at first, but I recognise your voice.'

'It was me at the fair, yes, but I'm not really Madame Zara. That's my grandmother. I was standing in for her when you and your—when you and Mr Kendrick arrived.'

Awed surprise showed clearly on Mandy Jenner's face as she sat back down on the sofa. 'How did you know who he was?'

Sasha had to restrain the urge to laugh. Kendrick hadn't been far wrong when he described his girlfriend as a fortune-teller's dream. She was so ready to be impressed that it was almost cruel to disillusion her.

'There's no magic about that, I'm afraid. Nothing much happens in a village this size without everybody getting to hear about it; so when I heard he was "in television" and you'd called him Dirk, I just put two and two together. I'm in that line myself, so the name was familiar. I wouldn't have thought filming the Horley fair was much in his line, though.'

The other girl stared intently at her for a few moments, then gave a little crow of triumph. 'Of course! I knew I'd seen you somewhere before—before today, I mean. You're Sasha Dinwoodie, aren't you? You're on that series about predicting the future—*Foresight*, isn't it? They're really interesting; I think I've seen all of them so far. You never said on the programme that you were psychic, though.'

The word made Sasha wince, as it always did. 'Well, I'm not really sure that's how I'd describe myself, to be honest. And I was just the presenter; I wanted to stay objective. But can I get you a drink? Or a cup of tea?'

'Well, I don't want to be any trouble...'

Sasha smiled. 'There's a bottle of wine open in the fridge, and I was just planning to have a glass myself. In fact, would you mind if I ate while we talked? Or you can have some if you'd like; there's plenty there for two.'

'Well, if you're sure... I'm starving, actually. What is it?'

The temptation was too much for Sasha to resist. 'Baked hedgehog,' she said gravely—and saw the flash of horrified belief before it dawned on Mandy that her leg was being pulled. 'No, actually it's just lasagne. OK?'

'Lovely.' Mandy grinned back, and Sasha realised with pleasure that she was looking forward to the other girl's company. She had opened the door expecting a confrontation. And instead she had found a friend.

*   *   *

'So you really are a gypsy? And your grand-mother's a witch?'

Sasha refilled her guest's glass before she replied. 'Half a gypsy. My father was a Gorgio—that's the Romany for a non-gypsy. Less than half, really, as I've never actually lived the life. If it wasn't that I've always been so close to Gran, even though we didn't see much of each other, I don't suppose I'd be aware of my gypsy side at all.'

'But she is a witch?' Mandy persisted, her eyes sparkling with interest.

'A *chovihanni*,' Sasha corrected. 'It's closer to the old idea of a "wise woman" than a witch as such. She doesn't dance naked round churchyards or perform strange ceremonies with cockerels or anything like that. But she does make charms for people, and she knows a lot about herbal medicine. And she has the Sight—that's quite genuine. All the women in our family have had it, to a greater or lesser extent. My mother had it, although she refused to acknowledge it, and I've got a touch of it—as you saw this afternoon. Only Gran is the real thing.'

'How do you mean? What you did seemed real enough to me. I'm afraid Dirk will never admit it, but I think you probably saved our lives.'

'Yes, but with me, it's just odd flashes, like this afternoon—and today was much stronger and clearer than I've ever felt before. But I can't control it or make it happen. Whereas with Gran, it's there in the background all the time; like a sort of super-developed intuition.'

'But you can read palms?'

'Well, yes; palms and cards and tea-leaves. She taught me to do it as a child, and technically I'm quite proficient. But Gran's readings go much deeper; she really sees things.' Although she's not averse to loading the dice to suit herself, she nearly added, remembering the King of Swords and the old woman's highly idiosyncratic interpretation.

'Well, I think it's absolutely fascinating. What sort of charms does your grandmother make? Good luck charms?'

'That sort of thing. For protection against accidents, or to stop your husband running round with other women or whatever. I saw her make one once, a "calling bag", for a woman whose husband had left her. It was a little leather bag, tied up with some of his hair. The woman had to carry it next to her heart during the day and put it under her pillow at night and it would call him back to her.'

'What was in it?'

'I don't know; it was secret. Lots of bits and pieces; it was quite lumpy and it rattled if you shook it. But if it's opened, the spell will reverse and drive the person away.'

Mandy was almost goggle-eyed. 'And did it work? Did he come back?'

'He did. But as he'd been leaving her regularly every six months for the whole of their married life, I doubt if it proves much.' She grinned as the other girl's face dropped in comical disappointment.

'I suppose it was your Gran who gave you the idea for the series?'

'It happened more by accident than anything else. I was working as a freelance journalist at the time, doing features for women's magazines and local radio, that sort of thing. I did an article on fortune-telling and that went down well, so I expanded it into a series of radio talks. Television would never have occurred to me; it was way out of my league.'

'So what happened?'

'Someone at Cotswold TV heard the radio series and thought it could work on television. At first they just wanted me to be an adviser and collaborate on the scripts, but luckily the director took a fancy to me and decided he wanted me to present it as well.'

'You must have been over the moon. There's a world of difference between working behind the cameras and in front of them. It's not often a chance comes to bridge the gap.'

There was a wistfulness in her voice that convinced Sasha she wasn't just making a general observation. 'Mandy... why did you come here this evening? Oh, I know you wanted to talk to me about what happened, but that wasn't all, was it? Or am I barking up the wrong tree?'

'No... although I don't know how you knew. Are you always so astute? Maybe you've got more of your grandmother in you than you know.' She smiled wryly. 'It all seems so silly now, having met you. I thought you were going to be Madame Zara, you see. I wanted to ask—to ask for some advice. You never got round to telling my fortune at the fair, and I wanted to know...' Her voice trailed off sheepishly.

'Well, I'm not Madame Zara and I can't promise to give you any advice,' Sasha said carefully. 'But

if you want to talk about it . . . Gran says that most
of the time, people make their own advice if you
let them talk long enough.'

'I'd like to meet your Gran. She sounds quite a
character.' Mandy paused, as if gathering her
courage, and then plunged ahead. 'Only I've got
to make my mind up, you see, and I've left it far
too late already. Dirk would be furious . . . but it's
such a wonderful chance. And it might even help.
I just don't know what to do for the best.' She
stopped to draw breath and looked at Sasha expectantly, like a dog that thinks it might be taken
for a walk.

'Hold on!' Sasha had to restrain her amusement.
'I told you, I'm not psychic. I haven't the faintest
idea what you're talking about. Why don't you start
at the beginning and let me catch up?'

'Sorry. I've been offered this marvellous—only
that's not really the beginning, I suppose. The beginning is that Dirk and I are—or at least were . . .'

Mandy's voice petered out. Her cheeks burned
with embarrassment and Sasha, watching her
fingers twisting frantically in her lap, felt something knot painfully inside her. Did she really want
to hear about Kendrick's private life? But it was
too late to back down now. She kept her voice
neutral as she supplied the missing word.

'Lovers?'

The other girl looked up gratefully. 'Yes. I was
going to say "in love", but I suppose he can't have
been. But I thought . . . Well, I'd never felt like that
about anyone before. He's a wonderful man. He

really cares about things; that's why he makes his films. And he was so marvellous in——'

She broke off again, her whole face flooded with colour this time. Sasha made no attempt to finish the sentence, although she knew perfectly well what the missing word would have been. But she quite definitely did not want to know that sort of intimate detail about the man. Tomorrow's interview was going to be difficult enough, without a bone like that for her imagination to chew on.

To her relief, Mandy seemed to regret her near revelation as much as Sasha did. 'Well, anyway,' she carried on in a more controlled tone, 'then this job came up, for a production assistant in his team, and I applied like a shot. It was quite a step up from what I was doing before—with Dirk, because it's such a small team, the PA's a sort of general organiser as well, you see. It's quite a responsibility.'

I bet, thought Sasha cynically. General dogsbody, more likely, if the way he was ordering her around yesterday was any indication. 'So what's the problem?' she said out loud. 'You got the job, obviously.'

'Yes. But that is the problem—or part of it. You see, when I applied, he told me that he didn't believe in mixing personal relationships with work. I said that was fine; I thought he just meant that we'd have to cool it at work, not make it obvious. People can get very bitchy... I'm sure you know how it is.'

'But he didn't mean that.'

Mandy shook her head miserably. 'As soon as I started—well, it was all over. Just like that; no

goodbyes or anything. That was weeks ago. At first,
I thought he'd be back once I'd settled in; that he
was just trying not to cause waves in the team. And
when we came down here, I hoped...' Tears were
running silently down her cheeks, her elegant hands
now clenched so tightly that the nails were white
where they bit into her palms. 'I left my door unlocked all night—no one would have known. I was
sure he would come...'

Mandy fumbled in her bag for a lacy handkerchief to dab at her swollen eyes. 'I'm sorry—it's all
got on top of me. There's no one I can talk to. And
I don't know what to do now, about the job.'

'You're thinking of leaving?'

'Oh, lord, didn't I explain that? I've been offered another job, you see, on a travel programme.
It's a marvellous opportunity.' Her voice began to
grow stronger as her enthusiasm took hold. 'Not
only would there be a lot of travel in it, obviously,
but I'd get to do some presentation too.' She made
a weak attempt at a smile. 'Places that no one else
wants to go, I expect—weekends at sunny
Rainwater-on-the-Mud. But it could be my chance
to break out of the back-room. It's the first step
that's so difficult.' Her voice trailed away again.
'Only it would mean losing Dirk completely.'

'Would it? Perhaps if you weren't working
together...'

'I know, that's what I kept telling myself. But
after last night... And he'd be so angry with me
if I left now. I'd probably never even see him again.'

Privately, Sasha couldn't help thinking that this
would probably be the best thing that could happen,

but Mandy was hardly in a state to appreciate such objective advice. 'But why should he be angry with you?' she said reasonably. 'He must see that it's an opportunity you can't afford to miss. Surely it won't be that difficult for him to find a replacement?' He's probably got any number of eager fans waiting to step into the breach, she thought caustically. 'When would you start the new job?'

Mandy's fingers started their frantic fidgeting again in her lap, and her eyes were fixed on them as she replied. 'That's the other problem, Sasha. I'm supposed to start tomorrow.'

'Tomorrow? And you haven't told Dirk yet?'

The other girl shook her head wretchedly. 'I didn't want to tell him until I was sure. And I never have been sure... I just don't know what to do.'

'But the other people are expecting you to start?'

'Yes. I had to give them an answer, and I thought if I said yes, I could back out later if I had to. But the time seems to have gone so quickly. I've made a real mess of this.'

'You have rather. Look, if Dirk Kendrick didn't exist, what would you do?'

'I'd take the travel job.' The answer was almost immediate. 'But he does exist, Sasha, and if I let him down in the middle of shooting like this, he'll go up the wall. You don't know what he's like when he's angry. I just can't face it——' Her face began to crumple again, but she brought it under control with a few dabs of the now sodden handkerchief. 'Oh, Sasha, what am I going to do?'

Sasha thought for a moment, then said practically, 'I can tell you what I think you ought to do.

I think you should take the job. There's no reason to think that you and Dirk are going to get back together while you're working for him, is there? So you're no worse off. And you know what they say about absence making the heart grow fonder; if you left he might even realise that he missed you.' And pigs might fly, she thought privately. But if her grandmother could bend the advice to fit the situation, so could she.

'But he'll be furious.'

'Furious in Horley. Whereas you'll be in Rainwater-on-the-Mud. He's not likely to break off shooting to come and tell you what he thinks of you, is he?'

'No...you mean, not tell him I'm going? I couldn't do that.'

'Of course you can. It's not going to help him to know that you're leaving at——' she looked across at the mantelpiece clock '—nine in the evening instead of nine in the morning, is it? Apart from giving him a chance to relieve his feelings? You can leave a note for him at the hotel and he'll get it first thing tomorrow. I wouldn't tell him where you're going, even; then you know he can't make trouble with your new bosses. By the time he finds out, he'll have calmed down.'

'Oh, Sasha! Do you think I could?'

'Of course you can.' A sudden thought occurred to her. 'You have got transport, I suppose?'

Mandy stared at her blankly. 'Oh, no! I came up with Dirk—I can hardly ask him to drive me back to London.'

Sasha sighed in mock despair. 'Are you always this useless, or is it just a phase you're passing through?' She glanced back at the clock. 'I'll ring for a taxi. You'll just make the last London train. Here—grab some paper and start penning your farewells; you can drop them into the hotel on the way past.'

Mandy grinned and took the notepad she was offered. 'Do you always work this kind of magic, Madame Zara?'

'Don't talk rubbish. You told me what you wanted to do; I just filled in the details. Dirk was right about you, Mandy; you're one of nature's mugs. Too gullible for your own good.'

A shadow passed over her face, and Sasha mentally kicked herself for mentioning Kendrick's name. 'I suppose I am, really,' she said sadly. 'I was so happy with him, Sasha. I thought it was all going to work out. I——'

'Stop thinking about it.' She reached out and squeezed Mandy's hands. 'One step at a time, love. You'll be all right; I'm sure of it.' And she was. An image came to her from nowhere: of Mandy happy, laughing—and pregnant, her body blooming with the same joy that illumined her face. And beside her a man, his face in shadow...

She felt her eyes fill with tears. 'Honestly, Mandy, I've got one of my feelings. It's going to work out, and that's official. Now get writing while I make that phone call.'

As she bundled her new friend out into the taxi, Sasha felt a quiet anger seething inside her at the insensitivity that had caused such pain. Crossing swords with Dirk Kendrick was going to be a pleasure.

CHAPTER THREE

THIS time, it was definitely the doorbell which had awakened her. And a bleary-eyed glance at the alarm clock showed no mitigating circumstances in its defence. It was half-past six; nobody went calling at half-past six. Not in Horley. Not anywhere that she ever wanted to live. For a long moment, Sasha debated the merits of burrowing back under the covers and ignoring the summons, but in the end curiosity won.

'All right, all right, I'm coming,' she muttered as her feet felt for her slippers and she dragged a dressing-gown on over her nightdress. Even June mornings could be chilly in a house with no central heating, and what the gown lacked in glamour, it more than made up in warmth. Armoured in its fleecy pink billows, Sasha made her way downstairs.

'Ted!' The sight of the village policeman on her doorstep in full uniform at half-past six in the morning was so incongruous that for a moment Sasha could hardly take it in. 'What on earth——?' Then, before he could speak, she noticed the expression on his face and her mouth went dry. 'Has something happened? Gran——?'

'No, no, Miss Sasha. Nothing like that. Only there seems to have been a bit of a mix-up...'

'I'll tell you if there's been a mix-up, Constable.' Another figure pushed forward from behind,

37

almost blocking the light. It took Sasha's sleep-fuddled mind a moment or two to place him, and when she did she could only stare up at him in horror. It was Dirk Kendrick.

'Good lord.' The piercing eyes swept her up and down with fastidious distaste. Sasha was suddenly painfully aware that her hair would be doing its normal early morning impression of an eagle's nest, and that the remains of the previous day's make-up were stinging her sleep-reddened eyes. And that pink had never been her colour. This wasn't exactly how she had planned their meeting... She waited helplessly for his next move, like a rabbit trans-fixed by a stoat. What on earth was going on?

It didn't take long to find out. 'There's no mix-up here,' he said curtly. 'This is the woman who broke into my car. And I have no doubt that if you remember your duty long enough to investigate it, you'll find she's behind the other damage as well. But I'm warning you—I don't intend to let this be hushed up simply because I'm a stranger and you and she are obviously on...friendly terms.' He made it sound like an insult, and Sasha saw anger flare in the constable's normally placid face.

'There's no question of that, sir. But we can't——'

'Then that's understood. I'll be back at the Feathers if you need any further statement from me.' Kendrick swept Sasha with a final look of contempt, then turned and stalked off down the mossy path. Behind the high hedges, his car pulled away with a throaty roar that shattered the early morning silence. Not until the sound died away down the lane did she find her tongue.

'What did he mean, "other damage"?'

'There's been a bit of trouble down at the Feathers. Someone's broken into his van and damaged a lot of filming equipment; expensive stuff, it seems. Now I know it's plain daft to think you had to do with it, Miss Sasha, but——' The constable broke off unhappily. 'Well, the gentleman says you broke into his car yesterday at the fair. I'm sure that can't be true, but——'

'Well, actually, it is, Ted.' Sasha was painfully aware how unlikely her explanation was going to sound, but she forged on. 'I had to do it, you see. But I don't know anything about any other damage. I can explain...'

But the constable's expression had perceptibly hardened. 'Then I'll have to ask you to put some clothes on, Miss Sasha. We'll need to sort this out down at the station.'

'But, Ted——'

'And I think for the time being, miss, you'd best not call me that. This is official business, and it don't give the right impression. Perhaps you'll just pop upstairs now, and get ready.'

Sasha felt her heart fluttering with panic. What if Kendrick decided to prosecute? What would they do to her? He couldn't... The constable must have seen her feelings in her face, because the official mask softened a little. 'Don't you worry, Miss Sasha,' he said reassuringly. 'I'm sure it'll all come out in the wash. If you've done nothing wrong, there's nothing to be afraid of, is there?'

Which wasn't entirely reassuring, she reflected ruefully, as she dragged a comb through her long black hair and tissued the dark circles from round her eyes. She might be innocent of the damage to Kendrick's film equipment, but there was no doubt that what her cousin had done to the Range Rover was strictly against the law....

'Miss Sasha?'

'Coming!' After a moment's indecision, she scrambled into the jeans and jersey she had worn the night before and hurried downstairs. 'OK, I'm ready, Constable. It's a fair cop.' Jokingly, she held out her wrists for imaginary handcuffs, but the policeman didn't even smile. And her heart began to race all over again.

After two hours in the cramped office of the Horley police station, Sasha felt as if she had repeated herself ten times over—and then had to listen to the same words being read back to her in the constable's ponderous tones. But at last she was free to go.

'There's been no specific complaint made with respect to the car, you see, miss. Although from what you say, there's no reason why one couldn't be made if the owner saw fit. It never does to take the law in your own hands.'

He looked at her severely, and Sasha tried to look suitably penitent. Inside she was fuming. He made it sound as if she had lynched Kendrick, rather than saved his life. Which, on reflection, began to seem like a far better idea.

'So, since I'm satisfied you weren't involved in the other incident, there's no more to be said. You be off, Miss Sasha—and don't go breaking into no more cars.'

Sasha was still seething internally as she walked down the little high street. How dared Kendrick have her practically arrested on such flimsy evidence? He really was the most arrogant, obnoxious——

A grip on her arm like a steel clamp half lifted her off the ground. 'What the hell are you doing here?' an all too familiar voice rasped. 'Don't tell me that that turnip-head has let you go? If he thinks. . . .' Sasha felt herself being dragged into the shadow of the inn porch and pinned against the rough stone.

'Do you have any idea how much damage you've caused? I don't know who you are, or who's put you up to this, but I'm damned if I'll let some bumpkin of a policeman turn a blind eye just because he knew your father! I'm taking you straight——'

'You're not taking me anywhere!' All her fury and frustration exploded in a yell that shocked even Sasha herself. In the hush that followed, every head in the street swivelled avidly towards the source of the excitement. Framed in the stone archway, they were the centre of attention. Sasha had to suppress a wild urge to step on to the pavement and take a bow.

'For your information,' she hissed instead, 'the police in this village work along the old-fashioned lines of arresting the guilty—not just obeying orders from any megalomaniac with a persecution complex who happens to get a bee in his bonnet.'

Her voice started to rise as she warmed to her theme. 'Thanks to you, I've been dragged out of bed at six-thirty on a Saturday morning, I've been questioned by the police, I've been accused of committing a crime I know nothing about—and now you've assaulted me in broad daylight in front of the whole village!' There was a rustle of self-consciousness among the onlookers, but nobody moved. This was too juicy a morsel of gossip to be missed.

'Playing to the gallery again?' Kendrick's anger had frozen to an icy calm. 'Well, you may be happy to stand here and make an exhibition of yourself, but I don't find it particularly amusing. Let's see how much you have to say for yourself without an audience.' His hand still clamped round her arm, he elbowed the inn door open and thrust her through unceremoniously.

'Upstairs.' Sasha's feet scarcely touched the carpet as he half marched, half carried her into the inn and up the steep stairway, past the publican and two startled-looking men who happened to be on their way down.

'In.' A key clicked in the lock and she felt herself being flung forwards on to something soft. A bed. Dirk Kendrick's bed. The voice behind her purred with menace. 'And now, perhaps, we'll start to get some answers.'

The bed was still unmade, and the rumpled sheets were haunted by the faint aura of his presence, a tangy, masculine scent that Sasha found disturbingly evocative. Scrambling up from the undignified position in which she had landed, she turned to face her captor.

'What are you planning to do—hold me prisoner until I talk? It shouldn't be too difficult; after all, only the entire village knows we're up here.' But behind her sarcasm Sasha could hear a note of uncertainty in her voice. Somehow, with Kendrick standing over her like a wolf over its prey, the idea didn't seem as far-fetched as it should have done...

'Oh, I'm sure that won't be necessary.' The voice was silky smooth, but the threat was still there. He picked up a sheet of writing paper from the dressing-table and flung it towards her. It fluttered to the ground between them. 'I found this waiting for me when I came back this morning.'

Sasha bent silently to retrieve the letter. Mandy's handwriting was as open as her personality, and as Sasha ran her eye down the script her heart sank. She sat down on the bed to read it properly.

Not a word of the new job—at least Mandy had showed some sense there—but a highly coloured picture of Sasha herself that cast her somewhere between Nostradamus and the Delphic oracle. Looking up at Kendrick's thunderous face, it was obvious that he had made the connection between his assistant's visit to the cottage and her subsequent defection. Oh, Mandy! Sasha wailed internally. Why did you have to bring me into it? I'm not in Rainwater-on-the-Mud!

She sat back down on the bed and glared up at him defiantly. 'She asked my advice and I gave it, that was all.'

'Oh, I'm sure you did.' Sasha could sense that his sarcasm capped a seething volcano of anger that might erupt at any moment. 'I don't know what you said to the stupid woman, but you must have scared her out of her wits. The manager tells me that she checked out last night. What did you prophesy this time, Cassandra—that the inn was going to fall down before morning? Rather inconsiderate of her not to wake me, don't you think?'

'Perhaps she thought that with a skull as thick as yours, having a pub fall on it could only be an improvement,' Sasha suggested with acid sweetness. 'It might knock a new idea or two into your pigheaded——'

'I can do without the insults. I just want to know why the hell you are so determined to sabotage my film. Perhaps you'd like to start by explaining who you really are, "Madame Zara", and why you were posing as a fortune-teller. You're no more a gypsy than I am, although with that colouring...'

There was a grudging note of admiration in his voice, and Sasha cursed the fact that she was meeting him unprepared. He might just have proved susceptible—and if she'd been properly dressed he wouldn't have dreamt of treating her in such a cavalier fashion. 'Dress like a queen and they'll treat you like royalty, dear.' That had been one of her mother's sayings, tested by years of small-village snobbery. 'Dress like a doormat and they'll walk straight over your back.'

But she had lost her chance to make a good impression, and the quickest way out was going to be co-operation. If not the only way—the door-key had disappeared into his pocket, and it might as well have been thrown into a lion's den for all the chance she had of retrieving it.

She adopted a tone of exaggerated patience, as if dealing with a particularly stupid bureaucrat. 'I was not posing as anything. I may not be a gypsy, but my grandmother is, and she asked me to take over the tent for a few hours. My name is Sasha Dinwoodie. Would you like me to spell it for you? Perhaps you ought to have it checked against the police computer. After all, I may have attempted to save someone's life before; this may not be my first offence.'

'Very amusing. Do you usually save people's lives by wrecking thousands of pounds' worth of video equipment and driving their work-force out of town?'

It took a major effort to keep her voice sweet, but she managed it. 'Mr Kendrick, the police are satisfied that I had nothing to do with the damage to your cameras. Quite apart from the fact that I would have no possible motive for touching them, the police say it happened between eight and nine last night. At which time, I was sharing a lasagne and a bottle of wine with a friend.'

Sasha felt instinctively that it would be a bad idea to mention just who that friend had been. If he realised how far her relationship with Mandy had progressed into friendship, he'd be bound to guess that she knew where the other girl had gone. And it wouldn't be easy to say 'no' to those compelling eyes.

'A friend? How very convenient. And no doubt this—friend will back up your story? And be prepared to swear to the times he arrived and left; if he did leave, that is?'

'No doubt he will. And no doubt the police will check.' And keep their mouths shut, please, Ted, she prayed. Had she made him understand how important it was to Mandy that her employer couldn't follow her tracks? 'But I don't think it's any of your business, Mr Kendrick.'

'No, Miss Dinwoodie, I don't suppose it is. My business is making films. Yours appears to be stopping me. And what I want to know is, who put you up to it?'

Sasha took a deep breath and had one more try. 'Listen carefully, Mr Kendrick. Watch my lips. I admit that I took that bit out of your car yesterday, inspired by some crazy desire to keep you alive. I admit that when your—when your assistant asked me for some advice, I gave it. Purely because I liked her and I didn't see why someone like you should be allowed to make her life a misery. But the rest is paranoia. I'd never met you in my life before; why should I wish you any harm?'

'I don't believe you.' His tone was flat and matter of fact, and it made Sasha want to scream. 'I've seen you before—I can't remember where, but it'll come back to me. Do you deny it?'

'Oh, no.' So that was what was bugging him! Sasha savoured the moment for as long as possible. 'I'm sure you have. It's so nice to meet one of my fans. Remind me to give you my autograph on the way out.'

For the first time, Kendrick's conviction faltered. 'What do you mean?'

'I mean that I have a television series running at the moment. And although I'm sure that the series itself is way beneath the notice of the great Dirk Kendrick, it has had a fair amount of coverage in the media. That's why my face is familiar; not because I've been skulking in corners, plotting your downfall, or whatever it was your fevered brain was imagining.'

'Sasha Dinwoodie? What on earth—oh, heavens, yes That fortune-telling tripe; I might have guessed.'

His eyes flickered over her, frankly appraising her. Re-pigeonholing her, Sasha thought cynically. Gypsy fortune-tellers broke into cars and damaged expensive equipment. Television personalities didn't. His scrutiny made her feel acutely uncomfortable, but when his eyes had finished their insolent voyage over her body he had a faint smile on his lips.

'You can hardly blame me for not recognising you, Miss Dinwoodie. You look—different, in the flesh. Especially first thing in the morning.' His smile mocked her confusion, and Sasha felt her face burning as she remembered how she must have appeared.

'It was the middle of the night, and I wasn't expecting visitors,' she snapped. 'And you of all people should know that the camera can lie. Or are you telling me that your films are different, just because you call them documentaries?'

Kendrick settled himself down in the room's only armchair before answering, extending his long legs across the carpet towards the bed. Sasha crossed her feet primly, acutely aware of his nearness. Why did the blasted man have to have such a talent for making her feel uncomfortable?

Mandy's half-finished revelation came drifting treacherously into her thoughts. 'So marvellous in—— ' Bed, she had been going to say. And his palm had revealed a strongly sensual nature. Sasha bit her lip and tried to banish the image which that brought to mind. His hand against her skin ... He was staring at her. Could he see ...? No, that was impossible. But why didn't he say something?

'Well?' she prompted, deliberately needling. She had been safer with his anger. 'Are you saying that you always show the plain, unvarnished truth? That there's no make-up girl hovering in case the tears get out of control, or fail to arrive on cue?'

'No, I'm not saying that,' he said at last. 'Although, in fact, that's rarely necessary. But at least my films have a purpose.' He looked at Sasha with a hint of contempt. 'The episode of *Foresight* I saw was about reading tea-leaves. Surely not even you can take that seriously? I doubt if most of the audience had ever seen a tea-leaf; and the most full-blooded of gypsies would have problems reading the secrets of the universe in a soggy tea-bag.'

Sasha swallowed her irritation at his patronising tone. At least he was no longer openly hostile; she owed it to her grandmother to try and use the opportunity their meeting offered. 'Very amusing,' she said drily. 'So what's the great purpose behind filming the Horley fair? I wouldn't have thought you'd be interested in our bucolic pleasures.'

'I'm not. But I am interested in the people who bring it here: gypsies, fair people, tinkers and so on. It's a whole sub-culture; and yet most people are hardly aware that it exists. I'm making a documentary about Travellers in Britain today.' He shrugged. 'Or at least, that's what I'm trying to do. I haven't had a lot of co-operation; they're a suspicious lot. And now, with Mandy disappeared and half my equipment smashed——' As if a thought had just occurred to him, he looked up at Sasha with a new light of interest in his eyes. 'Did you say that your grandmother was a gypsy? One of the fair people?'

'So you were listening to me, after all? I was beginning to think your ears were a purely decorative feature. Yes, I did, and she is. But I'm sure you wouldn't approve of her; she takes her tea-leaves seriously. She's a *chovihanni*; a gypsy witch.'

'Is she? Does that still carry much weight, these days? Surely the younger people don't believe all that stuff?'

Sasha shrugged. 'Some don't, of course. Or say they don't. But I doubt if many of them would like to put it to the test; Gran commands a lot of respect. If you met her, you'd see why.'

'I'd like to.'

'I don't think so, Mr Kendrick.'

'Call me Dirk. And why not? I'm serious—I'd like to meet her.' His voice was sincere; his face guileless. And Sasha didn't trust him an inch.

'Because I don't think she'd want to meet you,' she said bluntly. 'In fact, she'd already asked me to see if I could talk you out of filming the fair. I don't suppose it occurred to you that your "subjects" might not be keen on the idea of having their privacy invaded?'

'Oh, yes, it occurred to me. This isn't the first place I've filmed for *Travellers*, you know; most of it's already in the can. And I've had to cope with a lot of hostility. But what I'm saying is important, Sasha. It's for their good, and the good of their children. It's the Travellers' voices I want to be heard; and I don't intend to back down just because of some superstitious fear of cameras. Or for any other reason.' The words were edged with steel.

'I'm not stupid,' he went on. 'I was wrong to think you had anything to do with the damage last night; but I'm damn sure that someone at that camp was responsible.'

Sasha said nothing. From what her grandmother had said, he was almost certainly right.

'They don't want me filming, but they can't stop me. I'm having replacements for the equipment that was wrecked sent up by car. And this time, my crew won't be letting it out of their sight.' His grim voice convinced her that Mandy's absence hadn't deprived her employer of a chance to let off steam. Somewhere, a camera crew were licking their wounds.

'That's up to you.' There was no point arguing; Sasha knew it would only harden his determination. She remembered the stubborn solidity she had felt in his hand. The men who had smashed his cameras had put paid to any chance of persuading him. She would have to tell Gran there was nothing she could do.

'Yes. But it's up to you what happens then.'

'What?' Sasha jerked to attention, with the uncomfortable feeling that somewhere she had lost the thread of the conversation. 'What do you mean, up to me?'

He shrugged with an unconcern that didn't fool her for a moment—and a half-smile that told her he didn't expect to. 'I'm going to film, Sasha. That's definite. If they try to stop me, they'll be the ones to get hurt. I've got the law on my side and I won't hesitate to invoke it. They can't win. So wouldn't it be better for all concerned if they didn't try?'

'And you think I can stop them?' She laughed shortly. 'I'm sorry, Mr Kendrick——'

'Dirk.'

Sasha flushed. 'I'm sorry,' she repeated. 'But really, I don't have that kind of influence. Or any kind, come to that. I'm an outsider; if it wasn't for Gran——'

'Exactly. Your grandmother.' Kendrick pulled himself up out of the armchair and took a step towards the bed. 'She's the one with influence, acccording to you. If she told them to co-operate, would they do it?'

'Perhaps. I don't know.' Sasha felt flustered, pressured. His lean, dark figure seemed to tower over her, making the room seem absurdly small. 'But the question's academic; Gran's just as much against the filming as the rest of them. She'd never——'

'Not even if you asked her?'

'Me?' She should have foreseen this. It had been a mistake to mention her grandmother at all. 'Why should I?'

'Because it would save a lot of time and trouble for everyone? Because if things get out of hand, people might get hurt?'

She shook her head, on firmer ground now. The last thing she wanted was to save him trouble. 'Absolutely not. If you want to avoid trouble, don't film. I'm not involved in this, and I don't want to be.'

'Oh, but you are, Sasha.' His voice was softer now, and almost caressing. 'Deeply involved. I told you, I won't hesitate to call in the law. For *any* act of harassment I may have suffered.'

It took her a few seconds to realise what he meant. 'But that wasn't harassment! I was trying to save your life, you ungrateful bastard!'

'So you say. But your motives are irrelevant. Your actions were quite definitely illegal.'

'You'd be laughed out of court!'

'Perhaps. But whose career would that damage most? Pretty presenters are much more newsworthy than directors of worthy documentaries— and infinitely more replaceable.'

'You wouldn't!' But it was said without conviction. Kendrick held the winning card, and she knew it. She couldn't afford to call his bluff.

He smiled, knowing that he had won. 'Don't take it so hard, Sasha,' he said gently. 'I'm not asking you to do anything against your people. Just to ask your grandmother to help me.'

'And if she won't?'

'Then we forget it.' There was a long silence. 'Sasha?'

'Do I have any choice?'

'No.'

'Very well, I'll ask her. But don't get your hopes up; she's a very stubborn old woman.' Sasha stood up and looked pointedly towards the door. 'Is that it, Mr Kendrick? I should think the whole village is agog by now. So if you wouldn't mind unlocking the door...'

'No. There's another condition.'

She felt her jaw drop foolishly. 'What do you mean, "no"? You've blackmailed me into helping you, haven't you? What more do you want? If you don't let me out this minute, I'll——'

'Two more conditions.' He took the room-keys from his pocket and dangled them temptingly between them. Sasha made a wild grab, but he jerked them out of her reach at the last moment and she fell heavily against his chest. The next moment, his arms were around her and Sasha felt her heart fluttering desperately against him, like a trapped bird against a window. The hard metal of the key dug into her back.

'Let go of me, you——'

'Three more conditions. And counting.'

'All right!' She could feel the strength of his body through his shirt, and smell the same tantalisingly masculine scent as had clung to the crumpled sheets. And she could feel her own response... She tried to push away before he could notice the effect he was having on her, but his arms were like a ring of steel, binding them intimately together. She could hear the tremor in her voice as she attempted a feeble defiance. 'What are these conditions, then?'

He laughed softly. 'Don't worry, little gypsy. They're all very easy. One, call me Dirk. Only my bank manager calls me Mr Kendrick, and he's not nearly as pretty as you. Two, have dinner with me tonight.' She didn't reply and he pulled her closer, almost painfully close. 'Say, "Yes, Dirk."'

All that mattered was to get away. Her skin seemed to be on fire where she was crushed against him, and his scent was acting on her like a drug, making her feel light-headed and slightly muzzy. Just get it over with, she thought wildly. You don't have to go through with it later.

'Yes, Dirk.' She fought to keep her voice light, to treat it as a joke. 'And number three?'

'This is number three.' As his mouth came down on hers, she felt a flood of desire swamping her senses, setting a flame to the touch-paper which had been smouldering since he first touched her. And with it came the realisation that she had known it would end like this. And that she had wanted it to happen.

CHAPTER FOUR

DIRK'S lips were like his hands: full and sensual with a hidden strength that left no room for argument. But Sasha had run out of arguments. Her own lips parted voluntarily as he caressed her mouth: accepting, responding, returning his passion with her own. She had started as his prisoner, but at last it was he who drew back, pushing her gently away by the shoulders, leaving her dazed and bereft.

'Well——' Dirk was breathing heavily and his forehead was beaded with moisture. 'You are full of surprises, little gypsy.'

His words recalled Sasha to her senses, and she stared up at him, suddenly aware of what she had done—of what she had let him do. She had abandoned all her defences; all that was left was attack.

'I'm not your little gypsy,' she snapped, shrugging his hands from her shoulders and taking a step back. 'You asked; you got. Now, are there any other obstacles in this race, or are we on the home stretch? Because if that's it, I'd like the keys to this room, Mr Kendrick.'

'Dirk.' His eyes narrowed dangerously and the steel was back in his voice. 'Remember it. And I hope you don't intend to forget the rest of our agreement so quickly. Because if you do...You're a very cool young lady, Sasha, but don't ever assume I'm bluffing. I don't make threats I'm not prepared to follow through.'

'I'm sure you don't—Dirk.' She forced a smile. 'Now, the keys?' Once out of this room, she might be able to think. 'If I'm going to see Gran, it would be best to catch her before lunch. And I'll have to walk back home to get my van.'

He shook his head, and Sasha felt a momentary tremor of panic until he went on. 'I'll drive you down.'

That was the last thing she wanted. 'No, that's all right. I'll need to change before I go down there anyway. My grandmother's ideas are old-fashioned when it comes to women's dress. She doesn't approve of jeans.'

'Then I'll drive you home first.'

'Oh, no, don't bother. I can——'

'Sasha, I'm not offering. I'm telling you that I'll drive you home to change and then we'll go to see your grandmother. Together. There are ways and ways of asking a question, and I intend to be with you when you ask this one. Or you might—purely accidentally, of course—give her the impression that you didn't really want a favourable answer.'

This was so close to what she had intended that Sasha felt her cheeks redden. 'She won't believe me, anyway,' she said shortly, to cover her embarrassment. 'Why should I come pleading your case? It doesn't ring true.'

'Then you'll just have to be very convincing, won't you?' He tossed her the key. Sasha seized it gratefully and hurried over to the door. 'If you're stuck, I can think of one good reason for your conversion...' Behind her, she could hear him laughing softly. 'You could pretend to have been bowled over by my magnetic personality.'

'No, thank you. I'm not that good an actress.' Sasha's fingers were shaking as she tried to fit the key into the lock.

'No? You mean you weren't acting?'

'Oh—go to hell!' At last the key turned. She wrenched the door open and almost fell out into the corridor.

Sasha led the way towards her grandmother's trailer, acutely aware that for the second time that morning she and Dirk were the centre of attention. The camp was full of eyes, and she couldn't help wondering how much the watchers knew about her clash with her grandmother the day before. Were she and Dirk being weighed up as potential lovers? The thought was disturbing.

She paused a moment by the trailer steps and turned back to her companion. 'At least wait here while I tell her who you are.'

He shook his head. 'She'll find out soon enough. If she doesn't know already,' he added sarcastically. 'I thought she was supposed to be a witch. Just get on with it, Sasha, before I lose my patience. And remember—make it convincing.'

'Gran?' Sasha tapped on the side of the caravan. 'It's me.' The door was pulled open almost at once, and her grandmother's wrinkled face peered out, beaming with welcome. 'Come in, *kushti*, I've got the kettle on ready. Don't keep Mr Kendrick waiting in the cold.'

Dirk shot her a suspicious glance and Sasha hid a smile. No one entered a gypsy camp unannounced. And the old lady wouldn't need her Sight to guess the identity of her granddaughter's Gorgio companion.

Inside, she had indulged in another piece of showmanship. Three cups and saucers stood ready on a tray. 'Sit you down, now.' She gestured towards the velvet settle which ran down one side of the trailer.

Dirk folded his tall frame gingerly in behind the table. 'If you've warned her, our agreement is null and void,' he muttered at Sasha under his breath. 'I knew I shouldn't have let you out of my sight back at the cottage. I suppose you rang through to the site—I should have thought of that.'

'I did nothing of the sort,' she whispered back indignantly, her irritation fuelled by the fact that the idea hadn't occurred to her, either. 'And if you think you're going wriggle out of it like that——'

'Quarrelling already, *kushti*?' Her grandmother set the teapot down on the table and took her place opposite. ''Tis early days for that. Though I remember your mother; she had a tongue on her when your father was courting her——'

'Gran!' Sasha felt her face redden hotly. Damn, damn, damn. This was going to confirm all her grandmother's suspicions—and, from the look of enjoyment on Dirk's face, he had no intention of helping her out. Well, let him laugh while he could. If he thought she was going to meekly do his bidding, he was in for a disappointment. She still had a joker up her sleeve.

She took a deep breath and dived into her explanation. 'Gran, I asked Mr Kendrick——'

'Oh, don't let's stand on ceremony, darling.' He smiled at her grandmother—a hateful, deceiving smile, thought Sasha furiously, as she saw her grandmother smile back. 'All my friends call me Dirk.'

'I asked him not to film the fair.' Sasha carried on, through clenched teeth. 'But he says he has to. And someone damaged his cameras last night, probably someone from here, and he's afraid that if it goes on like this, there'll be worse trouble. So he wants you—that is, he asked me to ask you if you'd speak to them, make them realise they won't do any good like that. Ask them to co-operate.'

Her grandmother's face didn't change, but the shrewd eyes glittered inquisitively. 'So, he's got you convinced, has he, your King of Swords?' She turned sharply to Kendrick. 'Why can't you leave the people alone, with your cameras and your filming? They want none of it. Don't they have a right to be left in peace? Do we come and film you at your work, Mr Kendrick?'

'No. And I understand what you're saying, Mrs...?'

'Smith. Dolly Smith.' Unexpectedly, the old woman cackled with laughter, her wrinkled face crumpling in amusement like a screwed-up paper handkerchief. 'You understand, but you'll take no notice, eh? That's men for you, *kushti*.'

The moment was right. Dirk was smiling, his attention distracted. Sasha summoned up her courage and forced her face to stay calm. '*Pena naw*, Gran,' she said quietly and without emphasis. *Pena naw*, say no. Her grandmother would understand, and would know not to betray the secret communication. She just had to hope that Kendrick hadn't picked up any Romany during the filming he had done so far.

'What did you say?'

His tone was light and apparently friendly, but Sasha could hear the threat under its velvet surface. She did her best to feign surprise. 'What? Oh, it's just a Romany phrase. It means, "You're right there", or something like that.'

'Stick to English, girl—mind your manners.' No hint of questioning appeared in the old woman's eyes, although Sasha guessed that she must be consumed with curiosity, and her casual acceptance of the excuse was more convincing than any spoken confirmation. 'I hear my granddaughter was reading your hand for you yesterday, Mr Kendrick. But you'd not pay heed to her.'

Sasha saw with pleasure that it was Dirk's turn to be embarrassed. 'I'm afraid I don't really believe in all that . . . sort of thing, Mrs Smith.' Sasha knew he had nearly said, all that nonsense.

'More fool you,' was the tart reply. 'She has the gift, my Sasha, for all she's only half the Romany blood. And she was proved right, from what I've heard.'

'Mr K—— Dirk thinks it was just coincidence, Gran—Dan's accident happening when it did.'

She felt him shift uncomfortably on the sofa beside her. 'I'm sorry, but I still find it difficult to swallow,' he said apologetically. 'After all, I wasn't involved in the accident, was I? I'd have been more impressed if she'd told the man who was hurt. But I don't mean to disparage your art, Mrs Smith.'

He placed his hands palm-upwards on the table-cloth. 'I'd be honoured to have you tell my fortune, if you would.'

There was a moment's hesitation when Sasha thought the old woman was going to refuse. But she reached forward and picked up his broad hands in her birdlike claws.

For a long while she stared at them, unmoving. Sasha could feel the tension building inside her, and knew instinctively that Dirk was feeling it, too. Intellectually, he might not believe in what her grandmother was doing, but her presence was undeniable. There was a feeling of power about her that made disbelief an irrelevance.

The three of them sat as though turned to stone until suddenly the tension reached breaking point and the old gypsy thrust Dirk's hands back at him with surprising violence. 'Go on, then, since you must. Make your film; I'll speak for you to the people.'

Sasha was stunned, and she could see that even Kendrick was startled by the old woman's force. He was staring at his own hands, as if her words might be blazoned on the skin. 'Thank you,' he said at last. 'It's—I'm sure it's the right decision.' There was a long pause, and then, in a voice that only managed to be half-joking, 'What did you see in my hands, then? "Documentary of the Year"?'

'See?' The old woman's laughter broke the tension in the caravan as though a spell had been lifted. She stood up and started to clear the tea-cups away. 'What would I see? And why would I tell you, to be called a liar? But I tell you one thing, *rai*, one day you'll come back to Dolly Smith, looking for something. Something precious; something lost. And maybe she'll find it for you.'

She bent stiffly down and pulled out a plastic washing-up bowl which she placed on the kitchen work-top. 'Now be off, the both of you, and make your pesty film.'

Kendrick heaved himself awkwardly from his cramped seat and stretched. 'Goodbye, Mrs Smith. Thank you for your help. I'll try to be as unobtrusive as possible.' As he pushed open the caravan door and stooped to go out, the sun flooded in. 'Even the weather's decided to help.' He smiled. 'That must be an omen, surely? Coming, Sasha?'

'I'll walk.'

He shrugged. 'As you like. But don't forget we have a date tonight. I'll collect you at eight.' He walked off across the campsite, surrounded almost immediately by a crowd of curious children.

His certainty annoyed Sasha. But she knew that she would be ready at eight. Partly because he was ruthless enough to carry out his threat if she didn't stick to their bargain, no matter how unethically her agreement had been extracted. But also because she wanted a chance to redress the balance between them. So far, he had always caught her at a disadvantage. Tonight, she would be prepared.

She watched him out of sight round the next caravan, and then turned back into the half-light of the caravan's interior. 'Gran——' She hardly knew what to say. Had her grandmother missed her Romany message? Did she believe that Sasha had wanted a favourable answer? 'Gran, why did you give in to him? They'll be furious, won't they? Was it for me? You shouldn't have...'

The old lady shrugged with wiry shoulders. 'The river flows, *kushti*. What will be, will be.' For a moment her eyes were clouded with what looked like pain, and Sasha reached out to her in compassion. But the old gypsy brushed her away. 'Get along with you, girl. Leave me in peace, now.'

Sasha kissed her on her papery cheek and followed Kendrick's path out into the fresh air. But the sun which had greeted him was already overshadowed by clouds, and to her dismay she felt the first heavy splash of rain on the back of her neck. Damn! She cursed the obstinate pride that had made her turn down a lift. Could she catch him before he left? Praying that the children would have delayed him, she started running towards the car.

But the Range Rover was nowhere in sight—and the rain was falling heavier by the minute. A distant rumble of thunder added to her mounting sense of doom. Without even the consolation of being able to blame Kendrick for her plight, Sasha set off back towards the village.

By the time she pushed open the door of the cottage and dripped her way through to the kitchen, wet, bedraggled and in a thoroughly bad mood, she had solved that problem at least. It had definitely been Kendrick's fault. If he hadn't insisted on driving her out there in the first place... And he must have realised when the rain started that she would hardly want to walk home in a thunderstorm. Any man with a scrap of common decency would have waited to give her a lift.

But not Dirk Kendrick. Sasha towelled her hair with a savagery that made her eyes water. Dirk Kendrick didn't know the meaning of courtesy—or decency—or any normal social behaviour. Dirk Kendrick dragged people out of bed at unearthly hours in the morning to face trumped-up charges, blackmailed them into helping him and then...

Sasha swallowed, her throat suddenly dry as she remembered what had happened then. And the effect it had had on her... She could close her eyes and still feel his arms locked around her, still feel that first touch of his lips. The way her body had responded instinctively to his touch terrified her. Nothing like that had ever happened to her before.

But that was precisely it, of course. Nothing like that had happened because people didn't behave like that. Like—she searched around for a suitable comparison—like some medieval lord amusing himself with a serving-wench. No wonder she had over-reacted.

And to have the gall to invite her—no, command her—to dinner! What on earth did he expect—that she would let herself be swept into bed as easily as she had let him sweep her off balance and into his arms that morning? Because if so—Sasha yelped with pain as she nearly scalped herself—he was in for a disappointment.

She tugged the sodden jersey over her head and draped it over the kitchen boiler to dry, then peeled off her skirt and tights. Underneath, her legs were an interesting shade of blue. Well, a bath would warm her up.

Her underwear had just joined the rest of her clothing on the boiler when the phone rang. Wrapping the damp towel around her, she stalked over to answer it with a feeling of *déjà vu*, and a lurking determination to be extremely unpleasant to the untimely caller.

'Oh...' It was Mandy, sounding rather bemused by the fierceness of her reception, as if the phone had bitten her ear.

'Sorry,' Sasha apologised. 'You seem to have a knack of catching me without my clothes on. Did everything go OK?'

'Oh, dear... I'll be very quick. Yes, it's all fine. Dave—that's my new boss—seems very nice. He asked me all about what I wanted to do, and everything. He says——'

With a suspicion that 'quick' to Mandy meant anything under an hour, Sasha butted in. 'Look, Mandy, I'm sorry, but I'm on the edge of pneumonia here. I got caught in the rain. Can I phone you back later?'

'What? Oh, no, I'm going out this evening. It's all right, I just wanted to say thank you. And I wondered if you'd heard anything. About how he took it. I don't suppose you would, but I just wondered.'

'Well, yes—actually I have.' Thanks to you, she thought grimly. 'Did you have to wax quite so lyrical about my talents in that letter you left? Your ex-boss is convinced I'm to blame for you leaving, and he's not pleased. In fact, that's the under-statement of the century. He's furious.'

'Oh, no! Sasha, I'm sorry! I never dreamt... Hell, I can imagine. What did you say?' A note of panic entered her voice. 'You didn't tell him where I'd gone, did you?'

'No, but I had to tell the police.'

'What?' Mandy's voice rose to a shriek. 'What on earth...? Don't tell me he's reported me missing?'

'No, no, nothing like that.' It was difficult to sound soothing through chattering teeth. 'It's a long story, believe me. But they might come round to check you were with me yesterday evening. You're my alibi. Mandy——'

But, once reassured, Mandy's mind had already returned to her own preoccupations. 'Are you likely to see him again? Dirk, I mean?'

'Well, yes, I——'

'I suppose if you're at the fair much, you probably will. Only, if you do get a chance to talk to him, could you tell him I'm very sorry to leave him in the lurch like this? And if you could find out how he feels... Whether he misses me—you know. I'd be very grateful. But for goodness' sake, don't tell him where I am.'

'Look, Mandy——' But her voice trailed off. There wasn't any kind way to tell the other girl that, far from missing her, Kendrick was already doing

his best to fill the temporary gap by dating Sasha
herself. 'I'll try,' she ended lamely. 'But don't hold
out too much hope, Mandy. And I must go now,
really. Before I freeze to death. I'll phone you in a
couple of days.'

She rang off and hurried upstairs, her still damp
hair trailing icy tentacles down her back as she
waited for the bath to fill. The discomfort was
matched by a nagging sense of guilt, as if it were
her own fault she was seeing Kendrick for dinner.
Which was ridiculous, of course; and yet——

She really should have told Mandy the whole
story. If she hadn't been so cold... But Sasha knew
that that was only an excuse. She simply didn't
know how to tell the other girl about the day's
events; she hardly knew yet what to think of them
herself. And, however she did it, Mandy would be
bound to be hurt.

Perhaps tomorrow... By that time, their dinner
would be over and he would be off her back. In
hindsight, it might even sound quite amusing...
Sasha lowered herself into the water and started to
weave a fantasy in which she told Kendrick exactly
what she thought of his caveman tactics. Tonight,
she was going to have some fun.

Five and a half hours later, Sasha looked round her
bedroom in despair. The general effect was of a
bomb in a fashion boutique, with clothes strewn
everywhere. Sasha herself stood by the mirror in
nothing but bra and panties and glanced, for about
the hundredth time that evening, at the clock which

stood on her bedside table. It was fourteen minutes
to eight and she hadn't decided what to wear.

But no, that wasn't quite true. She had decided,
several times. At four o'clock she had decided on
the red dress, despite the raised eyebrows it would
cause in the dining-room of the Feathers. Somehow
she had a feeling that Dirk would dress up for their
date, and she had no intention of being upstaged.

That had been the longest-lasting of her de-
cisions. It had survived three hours, until she had
actually taken the silky red fabric from its pro-
tective sleeve in the wardrobe and slipped it over
her head. And remembered that the wide sweep of
the neckline made it impossible to wear a bra, while
the soft, clingy silk jersey did nothing to disguise
the omission.

Somehow, under the studio lights, it had worked.
Television needed extravagance, reducing cari-
cature to portrait and understatement to mere in-
visibility. But tonight was different. She simply
didn't have the confidence to face Kendrick in it;
and it was a dress that needed plenty of confidence
to carry it off.

Since then, she had almost emptied her wardrobe,
but nothing seemed right and the rainbow pile on
the bed had grown steadily with her discards. She
checked on the time again. Ten minutes to eight.
And he didn't strike her as a man who would be
late for an appointment.

Sasha stared at the mirror, frozen in panic—and
then something seemed to snap. '*Damn* you, Dirk
Kendrick!' She had spoken aloud and the words
seemed to vibrate in the silent room like a battle-

cry. 'Why the hell am I letting you get to me like this?'

On impulse, she reached behind her and undid her bra, tossing it over to join the heap on the bed. From the mirror, her reflection looked back at her seductively: long, blue-black hair falling in untrammelled waves over her naked shoulders and curving gently around her breasts. The late evening light seemed to work some alchemy of its own, turning the glass to gold and making her pale skin glow like polished ivory.

It was like looking at a stranger. And she knew, in an instant's recognition that had nothing to do with vanity, that it didn't matter. That she could face Dirk Kendrick in a sweater and dirty jeans if necessary. But it wouldn't be necessary. She knew now what she would wear.

In the distance, Sasha could hear the purr of an engine, inexorably drawing nearer. Calmly she went over to the bed and began to dig down through the crumpled layers. And when the car drew up outside, as she had known it would, she raised her arms and felt the cool silk slip down, caressing as it enfolded her body, moulding its softness to her own. She had been right the first time. Damn Kendrick, damn Horley. She was wearing her red.

CHAPTER FIVE

'WELL!' The soft exclamation was full of meaning, and Sasha's heart jumped with a pleasure that disturbed her. But wasn't that what she had wanted? To take her revenge for the way he had treated her that morning? To tempt him a little, to make him lose that infuriating self-assurance—and perhaps give him a little taste of the medicine he had dished out to Mandy?

It was only natural to be pleased ... But the glow his frank admiration kindled in her had little to do with revenge, and Sasha was suddenly very aware that she was playing with fire.

Dirk stood on the doorstep, making no effort to cross the threshold. Looking at her. 'You're a very beautiful woman, Miss Dinwoodie,' he said at last. 'And what's more, you appear to be ready on time. Can you cook?'

'What?' His down-to-earth query broke the spell and revived Sasha's feelings of irritation. Surely he wasn't going to have the gall to suggest she cook him a meal? Well, if he did, he'd be disappointed. 'No, as a matter of fact I can't. Why? Did you forget to book the table?'

'No, I didn't forget.' He stepped forward into the hallway, sweeping a draught of cool air before him that bit through the thin silk of her dress and made her shiver as she closed the door. 'But if you'd said yes, I'd have known you weren't a real woman, after all; just a piece of gypsy magic sent to tempt me. No one could be that perfect.'

'Except the great Dirk Kendrick, of course.' His teasing made Sasha feel awkward, and she reacted with automatic sarcasm. He really was insufferably arrogant. And he was wearing a dinner-suit, for goodness' sake! She had to admit its dark, lean-cut lines looked superb on his tall frame, but for the Feathers it was way over the top, and he must know it. He had hoped to catch her at a disadvantage again—it was the only explanation. Sasha resolved not to make any comment. Thank heavens she had decided to overdress.

She stopped aside to let him into the hallway. 'You'd better come in.'

Dirk brushed past and Sasha jerked her arm nervously away as she felt her skin tingle at the contact. But if he noticed he gave no sign. 'Isn't that the dress you wore for the series—the one on tea-leaves that I saw?'

Sasha nodded, absurdly pleased that he should remember. 'I kept all the outfits, though there's not much opportunity to wear them round here. It's a bit over the top for the Feathers, I suppose, but I thought——'

'You thought right,' he butted in before she could finish. 'We're not going to the Feathers.'

'What? But there's nowhere else in Horley—except the chippie.'

'The chippie was fully booked, I'm afraid.' His face didn't flicker. 'So I thought we could drive out to the Bull at Chesley. It gets a couple of stars in the guide, so it should be reasonable. And it would be a shame to waste that dress on the Feathers.'

'That sounds lovely.' Sasha realised that she meant it. The Bull had a reputation for being very up-market indeed—and at least in Chesley she wouldn't feel that everyone was watching them. 'But surely you won't get in at such short notice? It's usually booked up weeks in advance. And it's a long way to drive.'

'Actually, I made the reservations a couple of weeks ago, as soon as I knew I was coming down. I had a feeling that the food at the Feathers might begin to pall. And as for the distance——' He smiled down at her, a hint of mockery in his eyes. 'It must be all of twenty miles. Are you afraid we'll fall over the edge of the world? You'll hardly notice it, I promise. And besides, I wasn't planning to drive back this evening—there's nothing you have to rush back for, is there? I've booked us in for the night.'

'What?'

So much for keeping cool. Dirk's amusement at her reaction was obvious. 'Separate rooms, of course. But if I'm to do justice to the meal—and the wine—I don't want to have to worry about driving back.'

He grinned at her palpable relief, but there was a predatory, almost wolfish, quality to his expression that Sasha could interpret all too easily. Her host might have booked two rooms, but he sure as hell wasn't expecting to need both of them. She smiled back, hoping maliciously that his room was small, poky and uncomfortable. A man as sure of himself as Dirk would hardly have bothered to spend much on something he never planned to use.

'So how does it sound, Miss Dinwoodie? Or do you have an early-morning Sunday School class to run?'

His tone made it clear that he thought nothing was less likely, and for a moment Sasha was tempted to refuse just to see the shock of rejection on his face. But she choked back the impulse. If she had to spend the evening with this obnoxious man, at least she would enjoy the meal of a lifetime as a reward.

'No, it sounds like a good idea. And I don't have any commitments; I normally spend most of Sunday morning in bed.'

She hadn't meant it to sound provocative, but as soon as the words were out she realised how Dirk would take them. 'That sounds just what I had in mind.'

He looked across at her with such blatant desire that she swung away in panic. 'I'd better pack a few things for the morning.' As she fled, she could feel his eyes on her back, burning in their intensity.

Or thought she could. But, when she turned at the top of the stairs and looked down, her visitor's expression was one of amusement—and Sasha realised furiously that once again he had managed to put her at a disadvantage. Well, that was the last time she backed down. From now on, she would take the offensive.

She riffled through her wardrobe, picking out a pair of white linen slacks and a neatly tailored blouse. She would want to look as cool as possible the morning after turning him down. And a night-dress . . . Her hand hovered for a moment, and then picked out her prettiest. Not that she had any intention of letting him see that particular element of her wardrobe, but it was as well to be prepared.

She zipped up her bag and hurried back down to where Dirk was waiting for her.

'Do you want your coat?'

'Please.'

Dirk unhooked it from the rack, and held it ready. Touched by a sudden devilment, Sasha slid her arms into the silk-lined sleeves, brushing her body against him with deliberate sensuality and swishing her long hair to allow the perfume she had sprayed on the pulse points of her neck to waft seductively under his nose.

The response was immediate. Dirk's breathing quickened and his fingers tightened on her shoulders. Sasha could almost feel the electricity as he bent towards her, his breath on her skin betraying his closeness. For a moment she was paralysed with a desire to feel again the soft touch of his mouth, to surrender to the attraction she undoubtedly felt.

But something held her back. 'He's going to hurt you, *kushti*,' her grandmother had said. But that was nonsense . . . He couldn't hurt her, not if she kept up her guard. Unlike poor Mandy, she knew exactly what sort of man he was under that dangerous charm. And she had no intention of becoming another of his victims. Avoiding the kiss, she slipped quickly out of his grasp.

'Hadn't we better be leaving? We might lose the table if they're busy.'

'I hardly think so.' He didn't seem discomfited at all, Sasha realised with annoyance. But then, it hadn't occurred to him yet that he wouldn't get what he wanted in the end. He thought she was just playing hard to get.

Well, let him believe it. Life didn't deny much to Mr Dirk Kendrick, but she was going to be the one who got away. Revelling in a delicious sense of power, she led the way out of the cottage into the summer night.

Sasha sat back and surveyed the small but discreetly luxurious dining-room, quietly pleased with the way the evening was going. The menu—in French—had been a shock, until she had noticed the English description of each dish given on the opposite page. It was just as well; her schoolgirl French would scarcely have coped with the chef's *nouvelle cuisine*, and she knew that she would have ordered blind rather than give Dirk the satisfaction of translating.

As it was, she had been able to consult her own taste as well as the frighteningly high prices at the side of the à la carte menu. She was looking forward hungrily to her choice—and to the look on Dirk's face when he was presented with the bill. Sasha sipped the champagne *framboise* she had ordered as an aperitif, enjoying its raspberry sweetness mingled with the dry taste of the champagne. She could feel the bubbles tingling her nose, making her feel quite light-headed.

She glanced up to see Dirk looking at her intently. 'A penny for your thoughts,' she offered rashly.

'I was just wondering what the real Sasha looks like.'

'What do you mean?'

'I mean that so far I've seen you four times; and each time I've hardly recognised you. Yesterday, you were Madame Zara. First thing this morning you looked like nothing on earth—and then when I met you in the high street, you could have been about fourteen, with those jeans and no make-up and your hair scraped back into that ridiculous pony-tail. And now...'

'Now what?' Despite her determination to remain aloof, Sasha could hear the eagerness in her own voice and hoped that Dirk didn't detect it.

It was a forlorn hope. 'Fishing for compliments, little gypsy?' To her chagrin, Sasha felt herself blushing again as he went on, 'Now, you are a very lovely woman.' He was teasing her again; but behind his laughter was a hunger that almost frightened her. He was devouring her with his eyes. The consciousness between them was like a physical force, pressing on her... Sasha felt her breathing quicken in response.

'Dirk, will you stop looking at me like that, please?' To her relief, her voice came out just as she had intended: cool and with a touch of amusement. Not a hint of the turmoil that swirled inside her.

'Like what?'

'Like you were a cat and I was a jug of cream. I know the first course is taking a while to arrive, but when you invited me here, I assumed I was on the guest list, not the menu.'

Dirk's expression flickered for a moment, then settled into a smile. 'I'm sorry,' he said gravely. 'I don't normally devour my dinner guests—or at least, not before dessert. Shall we call a truce? Look, here's our meal arriving. You're safe, little gypsy—for the moment. If safety is what you want.'

'It is,' she said firmly. A plate appeared before her, and the waiter disappeared as unobtrusively as he had arrived. The food looked beautiful as well as delicious, a pale island of lobster mousse floating in a coral sea of sauce. 'That and food—this looks wonderful. Almost too lovely to eat.'

'But not quite, obviously.' Dirk laughed as she picked up her knife and fork and pounced on the chef's delicate creation with unashamed appetite. 'Are you always this hungry?'

Sasha realised with relief that his attitude had shifted subtly. The awareness between them was still there, but for the moment he was prepared to let it ride. The emotional temperature had returned almost to normal. 'Since I was arrested before breakfast and kidnapped before lunch, I haven't eaten yet today,' she said lightly. 'And it's not often I get the chance of a meal like this—this place is way above my price range.'

'The series hasn't made your fortune, then? Or did you fritter it away on crystal balls?'

His eyes were smiling, and Sasha found it impossible to be irritated by his flippancy. 'As a matter of fact, I spent most of it on repairing the cottage roof. I didn't need second sight to know that the thatch was going to join me in the bedroom if something wasn't done. And besides, I already had a crystal ball. My grandmother gave me one when I was twelve.'

He eyed her curiously. 'What a strange mixture you are, Sasha. You take all this stuff seriously, don't you?'

She shrugged and said honestly, 'Half of me does. The Romany half. The other half isn't so sure... That's the penalty of being brought up half-way between two cultures, I suppose; I can't decide which half is me.'

'Will the real Sasha Dinwoodie please stand up?'

'Something like that.' She laughed. 'I think my trouble is that it's my mother's side I really take after, but I was brought up pure Gorgio. My father was a schoolmaster, and he was determined that his daughter wouldn't be tainted with what he regarded as rank superstition. He didn't even like me being so close to Gran; he thought she was a bad influence. But he didn't quite have the nerve to ban me from seeing her altogether.'

'And no doubt the fact that he disapproved probably made you even more determined to spend time with her.'

'I suppose it did. I virtually lived at the fair when it came to Horley, and I used to cycle over to see her when it moved anywhere else within reach. My mother used to cover for me as much as she could, but we had some terrible rows. I used to dream of running away with the fair, but I knew Gran would send me straight back.'

'It must have been even more difficult for your mother.'

Sasha looked up, startled by his perception. 'Yes,' she said slowly. 'Yes, it was. She loved him so much, you see. She wanted to be the wife he wanted—even if it meant turning her back on her old life completely. Even if it meant rooting out everything that made her an individual...'

She could hear the catch in her voice as the old bitterness came pouring back. 'When I was small, she was so alive, so vital. But she turned herself into a ghost—a shadow of my father. And it killed her in the end.' Her fingers gripped the starched tablecloth, her meal forgotten 'He killed her.'

'What do you mean?' Dirk's hand reached out to cover hers. Its firm warmth was somehow very comforting. 'You can't mean that, not really.'

'No...' Why was she telling him all this? But she couldn't seem to stop, it was as if a dam that had been under strain for a long time had at last been breached. 'Not literally; not legally. Not even morally, I suppose. We were on holiday—all of us together. On the coast. It was a treat for me for having passed my A-levels. And my father decided he wanted to go out boating.' Her fingers flexed involuntarily, and she felt his hand squeeze a little tighter in sympathy.

'She knew.' Sasha gulped back the tears which threatened to break through her self-control. 'I saw her face, and she knew what was going to happen. But he wouldn't have believed her—it always infuriated him if she said she had "one of her feelings". She told him she needed me to do some shopping for her, but she went with him in the boat. And they were both drowned.'

'And you blamed yourself for not stopping them.'

'I didn't realise... Not really, not until they didn't come back. And then I remembered her face as they left.' Sasha shivered. 'I don't think I'll ever forget the way she looked.'

'Poor Sasha.' Dirk picked up her hand, and cradled it between his own. For a moment, she thought he was going to kiss it, and her heart started to race under a whole new onslaught of emotion. But he just held it, as if it had been an injured bird. 'No wonder you were so upset when I wouldn't take you seriously yesterday. I'm sorry, I shouldn't have been so blunt.'

She shrugged. 'You didn't believe me. I suppose there's no reason why you should.' She looked up into his eyes with a kind of challenge. 'You still don't, do you?'

He held her gaze for a moment, then shook his head. 'No, I'm sorry. I realise now that you were sincere, of course. But I still think it was just coincidence.'

'Mr Coincidence.'

'What?'

'That's what I called you, to myself. Yesterday, after it happened.' She smiled across at him, her spirits suddenly lighter. 'Thank you for not humouring me, Dirk. And thank you for listening.' She felt suddenly shy, and to cover her embarrassment said impulsively, 'So what about you,

then? What makes the great Dirk Kendrick tick?
Why did you decide to go into films?'

Dirk looked for a moment as if he were going to
give some flippant answer, but then thought better
of it. His brow furrowed slightly, as if trying to
remember a long way back.

'Frustration, I suppose,' he said at last. 'I didn't
start out in film-making; I trained as a lawyer. A
barrister. I spent four years after being called to the
bar, pursuing some tinsel-wrapped ideal of justice.
But in the end, I realised that I was like the little
Dutch boy with his finger in the dyke—only in my
case, there were a hundred holes and not enough
fingers to plug them.'

'What do you mean?' A lawyer; yes, she could
imagine that. Those piercing eyes and that devas-
tating logic ... He would have been an impressive
figure in court—or a terrifying one. If he wasn't
on your side.

'I mean that for every case I could help, there
were a hundred or a thousand other people in the
same situation. I was just scraping the surface. Then
I got involved in an Open TV project someone was
doing, about neighbourhood law centres, and I
started to see the possibilities—that through the
media you could help whole groups, really change
public attitudes.'

'You sound more like a politician than a film
director.'

'Oh, I'd thought of that as well, but I could never
have stuck toeing the line as a party back-bencher
for long enough to get anywhere. And, as an independent, I'd have had no real power.'

'And now you have?' Power. Was that all it came down to? Sasha felt a vague sense of disappointment, as if she had opened a beautiful box and found it empty inside. For a moment she had thought——

'Oh, yes, I've got power, Sasha.' His voice was quiet, but there was something in it which made her shiver. 'Television is power. People let me into their homes; millions of people. They may not know my name, but my images are in their heads, shaping their world. Did you see my documentary on homelessness?'

'Yes, I did. It was...shocking.'

'As a lawyer, I could have spent the rest of my life fighting individual cases. That film changed the law—oh, not directly, but it was a catalyst. People stopped pushing the subject under the carpet. It helped create a climate in which something radical could be done.'

'Yes, I can see that, but...' But the way he described it sounded very cold. An icy passion. 'Don't you miss the individuals? The feeling of having helped a particular real person—not just "changing a climate of opinion"?'

He looked at her in amusement, then shook his head. 'Not at all, I'm afraid. I didn't pick my clients for their cuddly personalities, you know; most of them I didn't even like. And with the few I did, I couldn't afford to get emotionally involved. They needed my expertise, not my friendship.'

'Did it have to be a choice?'

His voice hardened slightly at the hint of criticism. 'Yes. It did. And one I wasn't too sentimental to make, Sasha. If you needed an operation, you wouldn't choose your surgeon for his bedside manner. You'd pick one who could use a knife.'

'I just don't see why you couldn't have both. Surely it can't be wrong to care?'

His expression softened slightly. 'What a romantic you are, little gypsy. No, it's not wrong. But it's inefficient—and so it's dangerous. Any surgeon would run a mile rather than operate on his own wife because he'd know that emotional involvement could cloud his judgement. Law is the same; so is film-making—the sort of films I make, anyway. Once you've decided what you're going to do, they all demand total dedication. And complete ruthlessness. As a lawyer, you have to be prepared to tear your own client apart in the witness box if it will win the case. As a director, you have to go for the shots that will count, no matter what. Even if your subjects hate you for it—because you know it's the only way to help them.'

'And if you're wrong?'

He shrugged. 'Then you're wrong, and you have to live with it. The trick is not to be wrong too often.'

What a strange man he was. Coldly passionate; a calculating idealist. 'Did you ever make a mistake? As a lawyer, I mean?'

'Oh, yes.' There was a rough edge to his voice and Sasha realised that she had touched him on the raw. In a way, she was glad; it was reassuring to know that his armour could be pierced.

'I've seen an innocent man go to jail, and known that it was because I'd chosen the wrong defence.'

He smiled wryly. 'We don't all have second sight, Madame Zara. Most of us just have to do the best we can in the present.'

He leaned back in his seat and looked across at her with lazy pleasure. 'Though I would be prepared to make one prediction. I'm going to see more of you, little gypsy.' His voice wove a throaty enchantment around her, and she felt her breathing quicken. 'A whole lot more.'

CHAPTER SIX

AS SHE sipped the velvet-smooth Armagnac she had chosen to round the meal off in style, Sasha felt more than a little dazed. And not just by the brandy. Although she had certainly drunk more than usual over the course of the evening, alcohol alone couldn't explain the way she was feeling. Or the way she had talked.

She stared at the empty seat opposite, trying to work out what was happening to her. Dirk had slipped away—to collect the room-keys, he had said. But his absence didn't seem to make it any easier to collect her thoughts.

What on earth had made her open up like that—and to Kendrick, of all people? A stranger—a man she didn't even like. Only how could you call a man a stranger when he knew things about you that you had never told another soul? And Sasha knew that she could no longer pretend she disliked him. Her feelings were far more complex than that, but she wasn't sure she had the courage to examine them more closely. All she knew was that she felt happy in a way she hadn't for years; and that she didn't want the evening to end.

'Time for bed, little gypsy.' He had slipped up behind her as silently as one of the well-trained waiters, and his words made Sasha jump.

'Oh, couldn't I have another coffee?' It was just an excuse to prolong their time together, and she knew she sounded petulant, like a child. But, like a child, she was afraid to let the magic of the moment pass.

Somewhere inside, she knew that the bridge they had forged was fragile; fairy magic that might have disappeared by the morning. Whatever happened to their relationship, they would never stand again where they stood tonight: innocent, on the brink of discovery.

Dirk bent over her and his lips gently brushed the top of her head. 'Come on, little one. We can have a nightcap upstairs. I think we're keeping them up.'

She looked around her and realised that what he said was true; theirs was the only table not cleared. 'What's the time?' she asked in puzzlement. It couldn't be that late, surely? All they had done all evening was talk.

'Your coach turned into a pumpkin nearly two hours ago, Cinderella.'

Two o'clock! They had been together almost six hours. *Six hours to fall in love…* The thought came from nowhere, drifting across her sleepy mind like a wisp of cloud in a summer sky.

Sasha shook her head to clear it. It couldn't be— but tomorrow would be time enough for thinking. She let Dirk guide her gently out of the restaurant and up the stairs. He hardly touched her, and yet her skin was so sensitised that every fleeting contact of his hand on her arm or waist seemed to set her nerves on fire.

He stopped outside a door. 'This is your room. Mine's just along the corridor.' He looked down at her, and Sasha could feel a tension locked in his stillness. As if he were waiting for something.

'Thank you for a lovely evening.' A shadow passed across his face, so briefly that it could have been her imagination.

'What about that nightcap? Aren't you going to invite me in?'

'I——' Sasha hesitated, warning bells ringing in her head. She ought to call a halt before they both got carried away—and yet she didn't want him to go.

'Just for a nightcap. I promise. If that's what you want.'

What did she want? She had known that she was playing with fire, but she hadn't foreseen that the spark of danger would flare in her own feelings. She ought to send him away...

'Yes.' The word was a surrender—to what, she wasn't sure. He twisted the key in the lock and ushered her inside.

'Oh!' The room was magnificent; too magnificent. Lush pile carpeting covered the floor and heavy brocade curtains hung at the windows, giving an air of sybaritic luxury. A huge baroque mirror almost filled one wall. But she hardly noticed the details. She couldn't take her eyes off the bed.

Plainly intended as a centrepiece, the four-poster dominated the room like the temple of some barbaric god. Sasha stared at it in dismay. If this was a temple, what was she? The sacrifice?

'Dirk, I don't think... Perhaps I just ought to get to sleep. It's very late.'

But the door clicked softly shut behind her, and when she swung round it was to find her nose only inches away from Dirk's shirt-front. She jumped back with a yelp of surprise.

He slipped off his jacket and tossed it over the back of an ornate, gilded chair. He was wearing braces, Sasha noted with fascination. It should have been funny, but somehow they just emphasised the breadth of his shoulders and the muscular strength of his arms and chest. And his bow-tie was just very slightly askew... She felt an almost over-powering urge to reach out and straighten it, but checked herself just in time.

'Don't look so worried, Sasha. I told you, I don't eat my guests.' He reached up and tugged the tie undone, then loosened his collar. She could see a few dark tendrils of hair curling against the white of his shirt. The sight mesmerised her. Not before dessert, he had said. And dessert was long over...

'Dirk, I——'

'I think there's some champagne over there. Or would you prefer coffee? Personally, I'm going to have champagne.' As if she had never spoken, he moved over to where an ice-bucket was standing on the bedside table. With one smooth twist, the cork popped gently out and he filled two glasses without spilling a drop. He handed one to Sasha and she took it helplessly.

'To a very beautiful woman.' He raised his glass to hers and touched them gently together. 'To Sasha.'

His eyes held hers as they drank, and Sasha felt something stir deep inside her: a warmth which spread through her body, mingling with the champagne bubbles. She watched, mesmerised, as Dirk reached forward across the space between them and took a strand of her hair between his fingers, winding it round and round into a glistening rope.

'It's like black silk; a waterfall of black silk. Have you always worn it long?'

She nodded. 'My grandmother told me that cutting it would be bad luck.'

'Not another gypsy warning?'

'She said that one day it would weave a net to capture my heart's desire.' Sasha laughed a little self-consciously as the old woman's words came back to her. 'I had visions of some sort of Rapunzel-type scene with the handsome prince climbing up it to rescue me from the tower. I'm glad now, of course. I'd never have the patience to grow it again.'

'And did it?'

'Did it what?' Unwisely, she looked up, and their eyes met again.

'Weave a net to capture your heart's desire?' The look he gave her was pure seduction, and Sasha felt her heart lurch.

'No.' Why did she let him torment her like this? She tore her eyes away, but his voice went on, caressing her.

'Not yet, you mean. Hearts' desires are shy creatures; they don't come along every day. And a net like that would take a lot of weaving.'

His voice was no more than a whisper, and yet it was all she could hear, its dark softness filling her head like the swirling of her own blood. 'You're a very lovely woman, Sasha. A very sexy woman. And you know it.'

His fingers tightened on the black cord of hair which linked them, pulling her towards him. Towards the bed. Gently he plucked her glass from her hand and placed it on the table with his own. Somewhere at the back of Sasha's mind was the knowledge that she had to resist, but much stronger was the urge to surrender to the gentle tug of his fingers, to the velvet magnetism of his eyes. Helplessly, she let herself be drawn forward...

She was lying on the silky coverlet of the bed, his dark face poised above her. His mouth tasted of champagne. Gently his lips teased hers, his tongue tracing delicately the sensitive outline of her mouth, waking every nerve-ending to passionate response. Her body arched towards him, but his hand twisted in her hair, holding her down. Denying her the contact she craved.

Instead, his hand swept the wide neckline of her dress down over her shoulders. The soft fabric yielded easily, slipping down to expose the pale mounds of her breasts. 'I want you, Sasha.' His voice was ragged with arousal and his eyes burned her skin, sweeping every shameless inch of her with their hunger. 'You're so beautiful. And I want you so much.'

But still he didn't touch her. Her breasts ached for his hands, the hard peaks clenched with a desire that was almost pain. Every muscle in her body was tensed, yearning for the closeness which he denied.

And then, very slowly, he reached out and cupped her breast. His dark hand lay motionless against its pallor. She stared at it, scarcely daring to breathe, knowing instinctively that he was very near the limits of his control, that in moments she would be consumed in the maelstrom of his passion. And her own. And then, from nowhere, came an echo.

An echo of Mandy's voice.

'So marvellous in...' She could almost have believed that she was hearing the words, they were so clear. And their clarity struck another chord in her memory, chiming ominously with something Dirk had said. About making the reservations a couple of weeks ago... And then she knew.

Sasha looked wildly around, but the baroque hangings of the four-poster seemed to mock her with their magnificence. His hand still cradled her breast, a dark spider against the ivory of her skin. She thrust it away in horror and scrambled off the bed.

'Sasha?'

'I'm not sleeping with you, Dirk.'

'What?' His voice was thick with desire—and edged with anger. 'You want it as much as I do, Sasha. Just look at yourself.' His eyes trailed lazily down her body. 'Come back to bed.'

She clutched the red silk protectively against her naked breasts and backed away. 'Maybe I just don't like being first reserve.'

'What the hell do you mean?'

'You know what I mean, Dirk Kendrick. You booked this room for Mandy, didn't you? You were planning to come here with her—no wonder you were angry when she left. Still, it didn't take you long to come up with Plan B.'

Sasha half sobbed, half laughed as the full irony of it hit her. If Mandy hadn't decided to ask Madame Zara's advice, she would have got exactly what she wanted. It would have been her slender body in the four-poster bed; her pale skin under his hands; her lips swollen with his kisses. And for Mandy there would have been no pangs of conscience to spoil things.

'I see.' Dirk sat up and ran his fingers distractedly through his hair. 'You're right, of course. I was planning to bring Mandy here. We needed to talk. She hadn't been happy and it was affecting her work. I wanted to try and put our relationship back on a better footing.'

'Don't you mean back into bed?' Sasha knew that she was behaving childishly, but she didn't seem to be able to stop. Her emotions were a tangled mess of anger and jealousy, clogging her throat.

'As a matter of fact, no, I don't. But if I did, would it make any difference? Sasha, when I made those plans, I hadn't even met you. I invited you out because I wanted to see more of you; the fact that I already had a reservation at the Bull was just a convenience.'

He reached out as if to draw her back down to the bed. 'I don't know what Mandy told you about us,' he said firmly, 'But all you need to know is that it's over. It was just a casual thing.'

Just a casual thing! Sasha felt the anger well up again at his dismissive tone, remembering Mandy's anguish. As if her temper had blown a fuse, suddenly all she wanted was to hurt him, to smash the arrogant self-confidence that made him so sure he was irresistible.

'And all you need to know is that I never want to see you again,' she said spitefully. 'Don't kid yourself, Dirk. I went out with you tonight because you blackmailed me into it. And because I thought it might be fun to give you a taste of your own medicine, to see how you liked being dropped flat the way you dropped Mandy. I was right; it was.'

For a moment he stared up at her blankly, as if she had slapped him in the face. Sasha felt a surge of triumph at having shattered his composure. 'I wouldn't take her place if you paid me, Dirk.' She used the words like knives, stabbing at him. 'In your bed or anywhere else.'

'I see.' He stood up abruptly and picked up the ice-bucket from the bedside table. 'I'll say goodnight, then, Sasha. Excuse me if I take the champagne. I feel like getting very drunk.'

Sasha watched as he stalked out of the room, then ran to the door and turned the key in the lock. Along the corridor, his door slammed. She was safe. And she had never felt more lonely in her life.

Next morning, Sasha sat at the breakfast-table, moodily drawing patterns in the pile of breadcrumbs she had accumulated by her plate. Her face felt tight and scrubbed, and her hair was drawn back severely into a knot at the back of her neck.

The neat lines of her shirt and slacks were as different as possible from the red dress which now lay screwed up in the bottom of her overnight bag. Along with the nightdress she had never worn. She couldn't expunge that other Sasha from her memory altogether. But she could do her best.

Would Dirk come down to breakfast? And, if he did, how would he behave? She could imagine the cold indifference that might have superseded his anger, more terrifying than his fury had been. He would be polite and distant, and he would drive her home in silence. And then she would never see him again.

Sasha sipped her coffee and tried to work out what had happened to make that thought twist her stomach into an icy knot. Twenty-four hours earlier, the prospect of Dirk Kendrick disappearing from her life would have been a matter for relief, not regrets. And the events of those intervening hours should have proved without a doubt that he was trouble as far as she was concerned. She had thought that she could play him at his own game; and instead she had found herself responding to his particular brand of heady male attraction as naïvely and uninhibitedly as Mandy herself had done.

She flushed at the image that brought to mind: of herself, half-naked and totally abandoned, almost begging for his touch. Until that sudden, vivid memory of Mandy's words had saved her from a mistake that would have destroyed her own self-respect. Only it might have been worth it, to feel the ecstasy his hands and lips had promised her . . .

Sasha stared blindly out of the breakfast-room window. Remembering. If she hadn't drawn back, she would have been lying beside his lean, tanned body at that very moment—or under it. The thought made her shiver. She would have known what it was like to be pushed past the barriers of self-control, to lose herself in a mutual explosion of desire... Never before had she felt such wanton physical need, and she knew that all her inhibitions would have crumbled before it. But to him it would have meant nothing.

To Dirk, the evening had just been another interlude. Whereas to her... Sasha felt cold inside. Already, she had let herself be drawn into caring. Already, the thought of not seeing him was like a physical pain. She had been a fool to think she could play with fire and come away unburnt. Her grandmother had been right.

A noise behind her jerked her attention back to the present, and she turned back from the window to see Dirk standing opposite. It was like seeing him for the first time.

The elegance of the night before had been exchanged for a pair of disreputable jeans and a checked shirt. He hadn't shaved, and the dark shadow of stubble made his lean face seem—somehow dangerous. His eyes were red-rimmed and he looked tired. None of which seemed to lessen the effect he had on her. As he pulled up a chair and sat down, she could feel the tendrils of desire stir inside her.

The silence between them was lengthening, and Sasha screwed up her courage to break it. 'How do you feel?' Her own head was quite clear. She felt almost sorry. A little physical discomfort might have clouded the pain she was feeling now.

To her surprise, Dirk smiled his response. 'Better than I deserve, I suspect. How about you?'

'Oh, fine.' She had been prepared for anger, or contempt—but not for this. Was he just going to pretend that nothing had happened? 'Dirk, I——'

'Sasha.' Dirk reached across the table and put his hand over hers, trapping it.

The contact sent shivers of electricity running up her arm. Damn you, Dirk Kendrick, she thought. Why do you have to affect me like this? She tried to pull her hand away, but he held it fast.

'Look at me, Sasha.' Reluctantly, she raised her eyes to his face. 'Sasha, I owe you an apology. I behaved unforgivably last night, and I'm sorry. Only I thought...' Dirk hesitated a moment, as if shaping his words with care. 'I'd got you all wrong, Sasha. I let myself be fooled by the image you were putting over—I'd convinced myself that you were as sophisticated as you looked. And then, when you pulled back at the last minute like that, and you said you'd done it on purpose, to prove some kind of point... After what I thought we'd shared—I was so angry, I could hardly think.

'When I calmed down, I knew I was wrong, that it hadn't been like that. That you weren't like that. That you were just afraid...'

Sasha jerked her hand away. 'You're talking nonsense, Dirk. Why should I be afraid.'

'I don't know.' Her hand was free, but his dark eyes held hers captive. Searching. Probing her soul... 'But I can guess. How many men have you slept with, Sasha?'

She felt herself flush dark red to the roots of her hair. 'I don't think that's any of your business——'

'My guess would be none.' Sasha looked wildly round the breakfast-room, but his voice was low and, mercifully, no one seemed to have heard the exchange. 'Romany morals are strict, aren't they? Especially for girls. My guess would be that that's one piece of her gypsy past your mother never threw away.' He looked across at her beetroot face and smiled. 'Virginity's nothing to be ashamed of, Sasha.'

'I'm not ashamed! I mean, if I was, I wouldn't be—I mean—— Oh!' How dared he? How dared he be *right*? She pushed the chair back with a clatter and stood up. 'You're such an egotist, Dirk Kendrick. Just because I wouldn't sleep with you——'

There was a sudden hush as the clatter of cutlery on plates stopped simultaneously across the whole room, and Sasha sank back to her seat in furious embarrassment. 'You just can't bear to think I turned you down, can you?' she hissed. 'Well, I don't need to be a virgin to resent being treated like some sort of after-dinner mint. I have no intention of amusing you for a week and then being left high and dry like Mandy.'

'Ah, yes. Mandy.' Dirk seemed more amused than annoyed at her outburst. 'Yes, I've been thinking about her. You wouldn't take her place if I paid you, wasn't that what you said?'

Sasha stuck defiantly to her guns. 'Yes, it is. I——'

'Then that's easily solved. I don't insist on paying you. But you're taking her place whether you like it or not. Oh——' he smiled infuriatingly at her outraged gasp '—don't worry, not in my bed. But since it was your advice that drove her away, it seems only fair that you should fill the gap. Especially since you're the only person within reach who knows anything at all about filming.'

'What do you mean?'

'What, Madame Zara?' He raised his eyebrows in mock amazement. 'Psychic powers deserted you today? I'd have thought my meaning was obvious. Let me give you a few clues.' He started to count them off on his fingers.

'One, Mandy's defection leaves me short of a PA. Two, I couldn't hope to get anyone else out here until the day after tomorrow at the earliest, and even that would be pushing it. Three, Sunday's a big day for the fair and I can't afford to lose more shooting time. And four, not only are you on the spot, little gypsy, but you also happen to be ideally placed to oil the wheels with all that lovely local knowledge of yours. Fate, wouldn't you say?'

'No, I wouldn't. I'd say no.' Now that she knew what he was after, Sasha felt immediately more relaxed. This she could cope with; there was no way she was going to let herself be drawn any further into Dirk Kendrick's plans.

He shrugged with an unconcern which made her instantly suspicious. 'Well, I can't force you, of course. But it seems such a shame to have to drag poor Mandy away from her lovely new job.'

Sasha stared at him aghast. 'You couldn't—how do you know about that, anyway? Ted promised...'

'Oh, don't worry. Your tame policeman was a model of discretion. But television is a small world, you know—and I have a lot of contacts. I spent some time on the phone yesterday; it didn't take long to track her down. Her new boss happens to be a friend of mine. And if he finds out she's in breach of contract...' He left the sentence unfinished, but the threat was plain.

'You're bluffing.' But, even as she said it, Sasha knew she couldn't take the risk. Where his work was concerned, he was just ruthless enough to do it... Dirk must have seen capitulation in her eyes, because he drank down the last of his coffee with a look of self-satisfaction and stood up to leave.

'I thought I could persuade you to see it my way.' He grinned appreciatively as she stood up, smoothing the linen slacks against her legs. 'I'll run you home to change into something more...expendable. There's a briefing organised at twelve; I'll introduce you to the rest of the team then. OK?'

'I don't seem to have a lot of choice.'

He looked down at her and a half-smile flickered across his face. 'Don't worry, little gypsy. In a few days it will all be over, and you can forget all about me—if that's what you want. But for the moment, you're too valuable a commodity for me to let you go.'

Sasha felt a pang of utter desolation. That was all she was to him—a commodity; something he could use. After last night, he had changed his mind about how he would use her, but she was still in his power and there was nothing she could do to fight him. Dirk Kendrick had won another round.

CHAPTER SEVEN

THERE were three sets of eyes fixed on her, none of them friendly. The sound recordist, a tall, lanky man somewhere in his early twenties, glared at her with undisguised hostility, looking ostentatiously away when she tried to meet his eyes. 'Stew', Dirk had called him; short for Stewart, presumably. Sasha thought with distaste that it could equally well have described some of the stains on his scruffy denim jacket, and turned her attention to the cameraman, Owen.

His reaction was different, but no less disturbing. He was older, and Sasha felt instinctively that such unfriendliness was foreign to his amiable Welsh nature, but that didn't stop him from making his feelings plain. He held her gaze disapprovingly until she looked away, touched by a totally irrational sense of guilt.

And to top it all off she could feel Dirk's eyes on her the whole time he was speaking, their cool amusement daring her to contradict his version of the situation.

'So as a special favour to me, Sasha has agreed to step into the breach,' he was saying. 'Of course, she doesn't have any experience as a PA, so she won't be able to replace Mandy completely. But at least she'll be there to make sure we all turn up in the same place at the same time and get fed with some degree of regularity.'

It should have been the cue for a polite laugh, but neither of the others even smiled. Sasha's attention flickered between their stony faces and Dirk's words of introduction, wondering why they should be so obviously against her. Was it just natural wariness at the idea of an outsider—and an untrained outsider, at that—being introduced to the team? Or was there something more? Dirk had made it clear enough that she was just a general dogsbody—surely no one could resent that? It didn't make sense...

She heard her name, and dragged her attention back to what Dirk was saying. 'Sasha—you've got the shooting script, but remember, this is a documentary, not an episode of *Magic for the Masses*.' His tone was joking; Sasha knew that only she would have caught the note of contempt.

'The script's just a framework; it's not written on tablets of stone,' he went on. 'If there's something that's worth catching, we'll film it and to hell with the script. And don't guess; if you don't know what you're supposed to be doing, then ask, OK?'

He glanced at his watch and frowned. 'It's nearly one o'clock already, so we need to get moving. And Owen and Stew—guard that equipment with your lives. Any trouble with the natives, get Sasha here to deal with it. We can't afford another bust-up; this delay has sent us way over budget as it is.'

It was unmistakably the end of the conference. Dirk gathered up his papers, folding them to fit the inside pocket of his leather jacket. Sasha watched him preparing to leave, feeling suddenly very much alone. It was as if with his change of clothes he had put aside altogether the man who had eaten and drunk and talked into the night with her; the man who had so nearly taken her to bed.

If only it were that simple. But she knew now that the girl in jeans and jersey who followed Dirk Kendrick from the room was the same Sasha as the woman who had tasted champagne on his lips. And, by the tightening in the pit of her stomach as she followed him out to the car, she knew that it wouldn't be easy to put him out of her mind.

The afternoon swirled past in a kaleidoscope of impressions that left Sasha emotionally as well as physically breathless. She had started with the half-formed intention of not pulling her weight, in the hope that Dirk would abandon his private power games and let her go. But the whole operation had been so different from her previous experience on *Foresight*. Smaller. More intense. And more intimate. Almost without knowing how it had happened, she had found herself being drawn in.

And there was plenty for her to do. Bombarded by Dirk's peremptory orders, she had operated clapper-boards, fetched sandwiches, poured tea, kept notes and even acted as an impromptu tripod, with Owen steadying the camera on her shoulder to catch a shot as they were moving scenes. All this as well as doing her best to avert the riots which threatened every now and then to erupt from the gypsies' simmering resentment.

She was working harder than she had ever worked in her life. She was totally exhausted. And, despite the continuing hostility of the other two members of the team, she was finding it increasingly difficult not to enjoy herself.

'Wake up, woman!' Sasha started back to attention to see Dirk waving a bunch of keys in her face. 'We need the wheelchair out of the van. Quickly, go on.'

'The what?' But he had already turned back to Owen and, gesturing at the squealing donkey-riders they were currently filming, was deep in a technical discussion about 'panning' and 'depth of field'. Which Sasha suspected was nothing to do with the mud which clung to her shoes as she hurried back to the vehicles. He couldn't really have said 'wheelchair'... But perhaps when she looked in the van it would be obvious what he had meant.

It was. Feeling like several kinds of fool, she pushed the folding wheelchair back across the churned-up car park to where Dirk was waiting.

'Great.' He bent down to speak to Owen, who was settling himself in the chair with the camera wedged against the back-rest. 'Now, for goodness' sake, make sure you keep them both in shot, OK? I want to make the point that the gypsy child running alongside the donkey is actually younger than the kid who's riding it, so it's important we get the faces.'

Sasha found herself staring with open-mouthed amazement at the unlikely scene. The great Dirk Kendrick pushing a wheelchair containing a fat Welshman with a camera across a muddy field in hot pursuit of a rapidly accelerating donkey... It was then that she finally lost her battle. She was having fun.

'OK, we'll call that a day.' Dirk pushed his fingers through his hair in a weary gesture that was becoming increasingly familiar. For Sasha, it evoked with painful vividness their quarrel of the evening before. She could almost see him, sitting there on that awful bed... He had made that same gesture then, as she backed away. In retrospect, it seemed almost touching. As if he had really cared...

But no, the last thing she wanted was to start feeling sorry for Dirk. Already, she was too much in his power. Try as she might, Sasha didn't seem to be able to damp down the emotional and physical response he stirred in her. Their eyes only had to meet, and her heart started to race. And if he brushed against her... Even the most casual touch left her breathless with desire.

Dirk showed no sign of noticing it, much less of any answering response. But it was all she could do to act normally in his presence.

'Let's get it all packed up, then,' he went on. 'Owen, if you and Stew take the van back, I'll take Sasha in the car.'

'Surprise, surprise.' Stew's sneering voice was pitched so that Dirk wouldn't hear it, and Sasha ignored the gibe. She was getting used to his jeering accusations of favouritism, although she was still no nearer understanding the cause of the crew's antagonism.

She watched as the three men worked swiftly and neatly to pack the equipment away, strapping each item in its allotted place in the back of the van to prevent movement. Dirk didn't seem to have noticed the currents of dislike which crackled between the members of his team.

'You'd better eat with us this evening, Sasha,' he said as he slammed the van doors shut. 'I'd like to go over one or two things before tomorrow.'

Her heart sank. The last thing she wanted was to have to struggle through a whole evening of the others' hostility, but she knew it was pointless to argue. If she had learnt one thing about Kendrick by now, it was that he didn't take 'no' for an answer. Obediently, she followed him over to the car and climbed up into the passenger seat.

'So what did you think of your first day on the other side of the cameras?'

'I——'

I enjoyed it, she had been going to say. But just then there was a loud report as a stone hit the windscreen and clattered down the wide bonnet.

'Gorgio whore!'

The ugly words ripped through the cool evening air like a knife through silk, and Sasha felt the blood rush to her face. Dirk was already half out of the car when she flung out an arm to restrain him.

'Don't, Dirk. Just leave it. You wouldn't catch them anyway, and it would only cause trouble.'

He subsided reluctantly into his seat. 'I suppose you're right. I'm sorry, Sasha. You shouldn't have to put up with that sort of mindless yobbery.'

But Sasha hardly heard his apologies. It had been one of her grandmother's people who had thrown that stone. Someone she knew; someone who knew her. Someone who regarded her as a traitor. It was a chilling thought. The pleasure of the day turned sour in her mouth, and she felt a surge of impotent anger at the injustice of it.

As she tried to fasten the seat-belt, her hands were trembling uncontrollably. 'What's the point of apologising when it's all your fault?' she burst out in frustration. 'Those are my people, Dirk; the only family I've got left. They know me; they used to trust me. Or at least tolerate me. It's taken me years to build up that relationship—and now you pick me up on a whim and shatter it overnight.'

'Sasha, I——'

'Are you going to let me go? Because if not, I'm not interested in your apologies.' Dirk Kendrick wasn't the only one who could be stubborn. Sasha abandoned her struggle with the seat-belt and stared blankly ahead, her lips compressed to a thin line of determination as she fought back the angry tears which threatened her. 'Well?'

'Sasha, I can't. I need you—you saw how it was today. And if there is going to be trouble, I'll need you to deal with it.' His voice was surprisingly gentle. 'Don't get things out of proportion, little one. That was just one man, not the whole tribe. And it's only for a few more days.'

His tenderness was the undoing of her. 'Oh, Dirk.' She felt the tears start from her eyes and then she was in his arms, twisted uncomfortably across the broad front seat of the Range Rover, with her face buried in his shirt-front and his arms around her, breathing in sobbing gasps the warm scent of his body and his jacket's leathery tang.

And she was weeping, not for the anger of one nameless gypsy, but for the years of loneliness, of non-acceptance. Of being neither gypsy nor Gorgio. Of being alone.

Sasha peered critically at her reflection in the ladies' room mirror at the Feathers. Cold water had repaired the external damage, and apart from an unnatural brightness in her eyes no one would have guessed she had been crying. But inside she wasn't so sure.

'It's all his fault,' she whispered to the girl in the mirror. Ever since Dirk Kendrick had forced his way into her life, she had been living on a knife-edge of emotion, exposed and buffeted by every storm. 'If only he'd leave me alone...' But even to her own ears the words carried little conviction. 'What's happening to me?'

Sasha tugged the elastic band from her pony-tail and let the heavy mass of her hair fall free. It was a mistake. The soft caress on her shoulders woke a host of memories. Memories that crowded in on her, suffocating in their vivid sensuality.

'It's like silk. A waterfall of black silk.' And his mouth, coming nearer and nearer. And his hand on her breast... Her image looked back at her from the glass, cheeks flushed, eyes bright. Hurriedly she tied her hair up again, brushing it off her face. It was time to go.

A glance into the bar revealed that the others had gone into dinner without her, and the small discourtesy infuriated her. If she was going to be forced to work with them, their childish behaviour would have to stop. She marched into the dining-room determined to have it out.

With a mixture of relief and disappointment, Sasha realised that Owen and Stew were alone— and had picked a table for two. Well, perhaps it was better this way. Without their boss, they might be more inclined to tell her what was bugging them. Ignoring their obvious lack of enthusiasm for her company, she grabbed a chair from the next table and sat down to join them.

'So what's the problem?' she plunged in without preamble. Owen's bluff face reddened slightly and he looked down, embarrassed.

The younger man just stared back insolently. 'Do we have a problem?'

'Oh, I think so, don't you?' Sasha's voice was cool. Dirk might be able to intimidate her, but this gawky young man had no chance. And Owen looked as if he was ashamed of their behaviour already. She had a feeling he might turn out to be quite a sweetie. 'I want to know why you're both treating me as if I was ringing a bell and shouting "Unclean, unclean." As far as I'm aware, we've never met before. Or did I upset you in a previous life or something?'

'It's just——'

But before Owen could explain Stew had butted in, his whining, nasal voice drowning out the older

man's soft Welsh lilt. 'Maybe we're just fussy about
our friends.'

'And I'm not the Duchess of Kent? Oh, come
on, Stew, you might as well tell me what it's all
about. I honestly don't know, and you're obviously dying to get it off your chest.'

There was a moment's silence, and then Owen's
soft voice said apologetically, 'It's just we were fond
of Mandy, see. And we don't like to see her upset.'

Whatever Sasha had expected, it wasn't this.
When she found her voice again, her anger had been
replaced by genuine puzzlement. 'What do you
mean?'

Stew's voice was loaded with sarcasm. 'Little
Miss Innocent, aren't you?' he sneered. 'Except that
the whole village knows by now how you and Mr
High and Mighty Kendrick are carrying on. No
wonder Mandy left—I'm just staggered he had the
gall to give you her job as well.' An unpleasant smile
twisted his face. 'Still, the film's over budget and
I suppose it works out cheaper—no doubt he pays
you in kind.'

The insult left Sasha gasping as if he had thrown
cold water in her face. But somehow she managed
to bite back the retorts which sprang to mind. If
her aim was to make friends, she would gain
nothing by leaping down his throat. And she realised painfully that his accusations weren't totally
wild. The unknown gypsy had leapt to the same
conclusions. And probably Stew was right, and half
of Horley thought the same.

'I think you've got the wrong end of a few sticks
here,' she said quietly. 'Mandy's leaving wasn't be-

cause of me, except that I helped her decide that that's what she wanted to do. I don't think she'd want me to tell you the details, but she'd found herself another job which she wanted to take up at short notice.'

She paused, looking down at the table. 'I know she...cared about Dirk. And I don't deny that I went out to dinner with him last night. But if you're suggesting we're lovers, you couldn't be more wrong. We can't stand each other.' She felt a flicker of unease at her own words, but went on defiantly. 'He's about the most arrogant, overbearing man I've ever met.'

'So why are you working for him?' The tone was one of interest, not accusation. Owen sounded half convinced already, and Sasha gave him a quick smile of gratitude.

'Not by choice, I can promise you. He virtually blackmailed me—because of Mandy, ironically enough. He said that if I didn't replace her, he'd contact her new boss and pull her back. She didn't give him proper notice, you see, so she was in breach of contract.'

Owen was stroking his chin. 'I see... It looks as though we've been jumping to conclusions, then. I'm sorry, love. We thought you'd pushed her out, like. Because we knew she was carrying a bit of a torch for the boss, so when you turned up——'

'Well, I don't believe a word of it,' Stew butted in aggressively before the older man could finish. 'She's having you on, Owen. Anyone with half an eye in their head could see there's something between them. Where was Kendrick last night if he wasn't with her, eh? Don't be daft, man.'

He turned angrily to Sasha. 'You must think we were born yesterday. Well, maybe Owen was, but as I say, I'm fussy the company I keep. So if you'll excuse me, I'll be off for a breath of fresh air.' And, pushing his half-eaten meal away across the table, he stormed out.

'Oh, damn.' Sasha felt suddenly depressed. Stew's accusations had been so close to the truth. And the gypsy's words... It made her feel soiled to think how close she had come to betraying her friend.

'Owen,' she pleaded, 'you believe me, don't you? I only met Mandy twice, but I really liked her. I wanted to help her. That's why Dirk took it into his head to push me into doing this job; he blames me for her leaving. But it was what she wanted to do.'

Owen looked at her appraisingly, saying nothing. Sasha's heart sank. It was suddenly very important that he should accept her story. But then at last he spoke. 'I believe you, girl. You wouldn't have hurt Mandy, I can see that. And I'm sorry I thought it of you; that's what comes of listening to gossip, I suppose.' He paused, then grinned broadly. 'It's the bit about you and Kendrick hating each other's guts that strains my credulity, but that's your business.'

'But it's——'

'As I said, that's your business. Don't worry, girl, Stew'll come round. He fancied Mandy himself and she wouldn't look at him, that's what all that's about.'

Returning his concentration to the heaped plate in front of him, Owen took a huge mouthful of shepherd's pie—then broke off in mid-chew, gesticulating wildly with a fork as he attempted to swallow. 'Hell, I'm forgetting. He left a message for you.'

'Who, Stew?'

'Don't be daft, woman. Kendrick. The man you can't stand, remember? It went clean out of my head, with you barging in like that. He said he wanted to see you after dinner in room number five. I think he wants to show you his etchings.'

Sasha aimed a playful punch at his arm, but he shook his head, grinning. 'No, I'm serious. More or less. He's got a projector up there, and the rushes of the other stuff we've shot for *Travellers*.'

'In his bedroom?' Sasha was apprehensive, assailed by the memory of what had happened in that bedroom... But Owen just chuckled.

'Don't worry, your honour's safe. It's not his bedroom; that's number one. As befits the boss.' He looked at her curiously. 'I thought you were up there yesterday morning?'

Of course, the two men on the stairs... Sasha flushed, then wished she hadn't and reddened even more. 'Yes—but I didn't notice the number. It wasn't... He dragged me up there because he was angry, not to—not for any other reason.' She stopped in frustration and started again, trying to ignore Owen's incredulous expression. 'He had me arrested, for goodness' sake; that's hardly a gesture of affection. I wish you'd believe me, Owen.

There's nothing between me and Dirk. Nothing at all.'

'Course there's not, darling.' Owen scooped up another forkful of mince and held it poised. 'Except about twenty thousand volts.'

CHAPTER EIGHT

TELLING herself that it was ridiculous to feel so nervous, Sasha knocked tentatively on the door marked 'five'. But there was no sound from inside the room. She knocked again, more firmly this time, then once more in mounting irritation. She glanced sideways down the corridor towards room one. Should she go and see if he was there? But if he wasn't ready...

A vision of Dirk Kendrick, clad only in a towel and fresh from the shower, drifted disturbingly into her mind, and it occurred to her that, even last night, she hadn't seen him less than fully dressed. The realisation took her by surprise. She felt as if she knew every contour of his chest, his back, those long, strong thighs. She could picture him perfectly; and yet she had never seen him without the barrier of clothes.

Except by touch. She stood frozen with her hand hovering over the door-knob as the memories washed over her, paralysing her. Her hands, trapped between their bodies in that first embrace, straining against the implacable wall of his chest. Her hands released, revelling in the crisp texture of hair under cotton; cotton over warm flesh. The brief, brushed contacts as they had walked up to her room. And the weight of him; the glorious, perfect weight of his limbs overlapping her body. Possessing her...

'It's open.'

Sasha stared round wildly, momentarily dis-
orientated, before realising that he must have come
up the back stairs. 'Oh—hello. I was just—I was
just wondering where you were.' He was still
wearing the jeans and checked shirt he had worn
during the day, but without the jacket. His hair was
rumpled back from his forehead and he looked
tired, and somewhat harassed.

Her hand went out without thinking, as if to
comfort him, and she pulled it back sharply. 'Owen
said you wanted to see me.'

'That's right.' He was looking at her oddly—no
wonder. She was behaving like some kind of lunatic. 'Shall we go in? Or are you trying to cast a
spell to open the door without actually touching
it?'

'Very funny.' Sasha pushed the door open and
clicked on the light, hoping fervently that Dirk
himself was entirely without psychic abilities. Particularly the ability to read minds. It seemed a safe
enough bet; her grandmother's theory was that lack
of belief caused any natural ability to weaken and
eventually atrophy. And disbelief was Kendrick's
speciality.

The room they entered was still recognisable as
a bedroom, but to Sasha's relief the bed was nowhere in sight. Instead, a sofa and two armchairs
were ranged in front of a screen, and behind them
stood a large and battered projector with a heap of
film canisters lying by the side.

'The cinema comes to Horley at last,' she joked
nervously, perching on the arm of the old sofa.

'Where's the popcorn? You can't have a cinema without popcorn.'

'Damn! I knew I'd forgotten something.' Dirk picked up one of the canisters of film and started to thread it through the projector. 'Did Owen tell you what I wanted to do?'

'He said you wanted to show me your etchings.' As soon as she had made the joke, Sasha wished she hadn't. If he thought she was being flirtatious——

But Dirk just raised an eyebrow and carried on adjusting the film. 'That sounds like Owen.' He hesitated for a moment, then went on, 'Look, I'm sorry about what happened this evening, with the gypsy. And I've been thinking—I don't have the right to press-gang you into a situation like that.'

He paused, as if waiting for her reaction. But Sasha said nothing. She hardly knew what to say. If he was going to release her from their bargain . . . Instead of relief, all she could feel was an absurd sense of rejection. *He doesn't want me. I wasn't any good* . . .

He smiled quizzically, misinterpreting her silence. 'You don't trust me, do you, Sasha? You think I've got another trick up my sleeve. Well, I suppose I can't blame you. But this is a genuine offer, as they say on the adverts. Only one string attached.'

'Which is?' This sounded more like the Dirk she knew.

'That you keep an open mind until after you've seen what we've shot so far for *Travellers*. It's not been edited yet, but it should give you more idea what I'm trying to achieve. I don't want to lose you, Sasha. You're doing a good job and I'd prefer you to enjoy it, if you can.'

'A willing slave?' she mocked, and felt a pang of remorse when she saw his face tighten. His un-expected praise had touched her—and his offer seemed fair enough. 'I'm sorry, Dirk, I was just teasing. I did quite enjoy it today, until—until it happened. And I'd love to see your film.'

'I'm glad.' Their eyes met and Sasha felt a treacherous warmth creep over her, but she couldn't look away. 'A truce, then?'

'A truce.' Sasha settled down contentedly in front of the screen. The lights went off, and as the pro-jector whirred into life Dirk joined her on the sofa.

'There's only one thing wrong with this set-up,' he murmured softly. 'We're not in the back row.'

But before she could muster a suitable retort the screen burst into life in front of them. For the first two minutes, Sasha was acutely aware of his presence next to her in the semi-darkness. And then the images took over.

Shocking, haunting images. Images of men and women embittered and hardened by lifetimes of struggle. Images of ignorance and disease. Of children with adult eyes, aged by hunger and cold and the poverty that had stolen their childhood. The pictures rolled out in front of her in a tapestry of horror, the disjointed, unfinished nature of the film somehow adding to the quality of nightmare.

Dirk hadn't restricted his film to the traditional Romany gypsies. *Travellers*, it was called, and all the modern nomads were there: those who had chosen the life set beside those who had drifted into it, unwillingly propelled by homelessness, unemployment or trouble with the law.

Shots of traditional gypsy crafts were set against pictures of a grey-faced prostitute, accepting a crumpled five-pound note while her baby squalled in the back of her trailer and a toddler clung to her skirts. Horse-trading at Appleby fair was contrasted silently with a desolate wasteland of rusting scrap. Firelit figures, half obscured by billowing black smoke from a pile of burning tyres, clambered on its surface like devils from hell.

And all the time the feeling of hopelessness, of being trapped. Always, it came back to the children. Subtly, the film's contrasts made it terrifyingly clear that all the children could look forward to was a bleak re-enactment of their parents' cramped lives, crippled by illiteracy and homelessness, shut out from a society that hardly knew of their existence.

How long the film lasted, she couldn't have said. But when the screen flickered white, then plunged them into darkness, she felt emotionally stunned.

'So,' his voice was soft in the darkness, 'what did you think?'

Sasha's answer burst out without thinking, without even knowing what the words were going to be. 'It's brilliant, Dirk.' The velvet blackness pressed in on her, waiting. 'But it's not true.'

She heard his sharp intake of breath, inches from her ear. And then a long, uncomfortable silence. Sasha braced herself for his anger, but when he finally spoke his voice was gentle.

'It's all true, Sasha. I promise you that. Every shot in that film really happened, and without any prompting from me.'

'Yes, I know—I didn't mean that.' What the hell did she mean? she thought wildly. It had been a gut reaction, not a reasoned argument. 'I'm sure the incidents are true enough. But the whole thing; the film itself...' She was expressing this badly, she knew, but it seemed important to explain. 'It's not the way things really are.'

'You mean it's biased?' He still didn't seem angry. It was as if the darkness surrounded them like a soft, thick cloud, cushioning and protecting them. Sasha felt her nervousness melt away. She felt she could say anything... All that mattered was to make him see.

'Something like that.' She seized gratefully on his shred of understanding. 'It's as if you made the film through grey-tinted lenses. Someone else could probably have done the opposite and made a film of glorious optimism—but neither of them would have been the truth. Do you see what I mean?'

'Yes, I do. And you're right in a way—but it's not accidental. I don't make films for fun, Sasha. I make them for a purpose. I make them to force people to see the things they would rather sweep under the carpet. I want to change things, to change laws. To do that, I have to shock, and I have to be single-minded about what I am trying to say.'

'Even if it's not true?'

He sighed, and when he spoke his exasperation was beginning to show. 'It is true, Sasha. It's just not the whole truth. As a lawyer prosecuting a bad landlord, I didn't waste time explaining to the court that he was kind to dogs and fond of his mother. I just told them that he kept his tenants in sub-human conditions and had them beaten up if they complained to the rent tribunal. Not because his good points didn't exist, but because they would just have clouded the issue.'

'But that's different ... He was guilty, no matter what his private life was like. But here you're not talking about individuals. You call it *Travellers*— you're including my grandmother, by implication, and all her people. Travelling is the only life they want; they're happy——'

'Are they? All of them? What about those children we filmed yesterday? Will they all be content to follow in their parents' footsteps, in a world where they're increasingly out of place?'

'Then that's their choice. My mother chose to leave; so could they.'

'Could they? Your mother could break free because she had your father to run to. What do you think would have happened to her if he hadn't been there? If she'd had to support herself? With no-where to live and no qualifications? A man might pick up some casual labouring job, but a woman would be lucky not to end up on the streets. Especially if she did what most of the poor fools do and headed straight for London.'

'But you're ignoring all the good things!' Sasha's voice rose in a wail of frustration. 'Gypsies don't want jobs; they despise that sort of nine-to-five slavery. They don't have mortgages, or rates to pay.

They're their own masters—your film shows none of that.'

She searched around desperately for the words that might convince him. 'They're an endangered species, Dirk. Can't you look at them like that? If you were making a film about the plight of tigers or something, you'd show them being hunted and trapped. But you'd film them free and happy as well, to show they're worth saving. That's all I'm saying. Or people will think, "So what? It's their fault—why don't they just settle down?"'

'I don't know why we're sitting here in the dark.' Sasha felt him move abruptly from beside her, and then they were both blinking in the blaze of light. He wasn't going to answer her, she thought bitterly. She was right, but he would never admit it.

'Well?'

He shook his head. 'I understand what you're saying, Sasha, but it wouldn't work. The film has to have maximum impact, maximum shock. Like *Homeless*, it's got to be the almighty kick that propels things into motion. I can't afford to dilute its message with a lot of happy-family stuff. I'm sorry, I know how you feel. They're your people, and the ones you know are the lucky ones. But I know what I'm doing.'

'Do you? I——' But a look at his face told her she was wasting her breath. 'Oh, what's the use of arguing? You've made up your mind.'

'Then perhaps you should stay on and try and change it for me.'

For a moment she was tempted. She had enjoyed the day's filming, until its upsetting conclusion.

And if there was a chance she could influence him to lighten his dark vision... But she shook her head. 'I'm sorry, Dirk. But you wouldn't really be interested in my views, would you? You just want an extra pair of hands and some free local knowledge thrown in.' She stood up abruptly—then noticed the clock on the wall. 'Ten o'clock!' They had been sitting in the dark for over an hour. 'Don't bother to give me a lift back, Dirk. I'll get a taxi.'

He didn't argue, and Sasha felt just a hint of disappointment. But what had she expected? They had only called a truce, not——

She glanced idly down at the film canisters on the table and froze into immobility. Each canister had a label giving details of the contents. And each label had a name blazoned across it.

Sword-King Productions Ltd.

For a moment, it was as if the world stood still. Dirk was standing by the door, his hand poised over the light-switch, waiting for her, but she couldn't move. And when at last she found her voice it was little more than a croak.

'What's "Sword-King Productions", Dirk?'

He looked at her in surprise. 'It's the name of my company. Didn't you know?'

'No. No, I didn't. What made you pick that name?'

He shrugged. 'It's a sort of translation of my own name. A dirk is a type of short sword or dagger, and Kendrick means "ruler of the people". I can't remember what put the idea into my head, but it seemed more memorable than "Dirk Kendrick Films" or something.'

He grinned and shook his head in mock reproach. 'Though not to you, obviously. You can't have been paying proper attention when my stuff was shown on TV. In fact, your grandmother's better informed than you—when you took me to see her that time, she called me your "King of Swords". Don't you remember? And I doubt if she's ever seen any of my films.'

Sasha said nothing. She couldn't. She had the eerie sensation that, for a moment, the walls of reality had become transparent and she had seen the secret workings turning away. Wheels within wheels. And the implications terrified her.

'Are you all right, Sasha?' Dirk left the door and came hurrying towards her. 'You look as if you're going to faint. Come on, sit down.'

He tried to guide her back to the sofa, but she shook her head, hanging on to the projector-table for support. 'No, I'll be OK. I'm just tired.'

'I'll run you home. Or would you like me to get you a room here? If you're ill, you shouldn't be alone.' His voice was gentle and concerned, and Sasha wanted desperately just to lean back into his arms and let him take care of her.

But somehow she resisted. 'I'm not ill. Just take me back, Dirk. Please. I'll be fine in the morning.'

'Not until you tell me what's the matter,' he persisted. 'People who've just had a tiring day don't suddenly go white as a sheet and nearly collapse. Five minutes ago you were giving me hell. What happened? You look as if you've seen a ghost.'

The phrase was so nearly appropriate that Sasha started to laugh. Only, having started, she found she couldn't stop. Not even when she realised she was crying as well. She tried to gulp an apology, but the words turned into hiccuping sobs. But Dirk didn't seem to be annoyed. For the second time that evening his arms were round her, holding her gently but firmly against him, one broad hand stroking her hair.

'It's all right, little gypsy. It's all right.'

Once she had calmed down, he took immediate control. 'I've got a bottle of brandy in my room. My prescription would be a large one—for both of us. And you can tell me what the hell's going on. And then I intend to put you to bed. I'll have the hotel make up another room for me.'

He swung her up into his arms, ignoring her half-hearted protests, and elbowed the door open. 'Not a word until you've had that drink.'

But Sasha had given up fighting. Her emotional storm seemed to have left in its wake a languorous desire to be cosseted, and she lay passively in his arms as he carried her down the corridor and into his room. Not until she was seated beside him on the bed with a glass in her hand and had taken a few sips of brandy did he let her speak.

'So tell me about it,' he invited, though it sounded to Sasha more like a command. 'And don't give me this stuff about being tired. There has to be more to it than that.'

It was just too much trouble to try and invent a feasible lie. To her own surprise, Sasha found herself telling him the whole story.

'So when she called you "King of Swords",' she finished, 'it had nothing to do with the name of your company. It was because of the cards.'

'I see.'

Sasha looked at him half-fearfully, expecting ridicule. 'She knew, Dirk. She predicted——'

'What? That we would be lovers?' He reached out and brushed his finger softly against the down of her cheek in a gesture that was at once sensual and reassuring. 'My cameraman's been predicting that since he saw us together yesterday morning, but no one accuses him of having mysterious powers. There's nothing magical about a knowledge of human nature, little one. Your grandmother is a very bright lady.'

'But when she laid the cards, she'd never met you!'

'But she knows you well, and she'd heard about our meeting. She could probably see the effect I'd had on you—— Oh, don't pretend, Sasha.' His finger trailed back across her cheek, tucking a stray wisp of hair behind her ear. Sasha felt a tremor of excitement follow in its wake, as if each tiny hair were individually sensitised. If it was meant to be a demonstration, it was a highly effective one.

'We've struck sparks off each other ever since the moment we met, and you know it,' Dirk went on slowly. 'And since we seem to have specialised in public performances, the whole of Horley knows it as well. It's hardly surprising your gran managed to put two and two together.'

'But the card was the King of Swords, Dirk! And now you tell me that's practically your name. How do you explain that? No, don't tell me. Coincidence?'

'Coincidences happen, Sasha. Every so often, outsiders romp home. That's what statistics are all about. And gambling. And fortune-telling, too. People like your grandmother just know how to take advantage of the odds; and I don't mean that cynically. She has a great talent, and she and her customers believe it's something supernatural. But it's not, Sasha. She could be wrong...'

Gently, he pulled her round to face him, holding her shoulders and looking down into her eyes. 'Although in this case, I think she was right. We will be lovers, Sasha.'

She stared up at him, mesmerised by his certainty, something deep inside her recognising the inevitability of what he was saying. His hands slipped up to cradle her face, and Sasha felt her lips part in unconscious anticipation.

'We will be lovers,' he repeated. 'Though not now, not tonight. But through choice, not some predestined Fate. Because it's what we most desire. Because——' His lips met hers, and Sasha felt her whole body shudder with an intensity of pleasure that exploded inside her like champagne. 'Because of this.'

CHAPTER NINE

'DAMN, damn, damn, damn!'

Sasha sat on the edge of Dirk Kendrick's bed, wrapped in Dirk Kendrick's bath-robe, watching Dirk Kendrick pacing back and forth across the carpet in fury. He had drifted in and out of her dreams all night, and now the sight of him in the flesh, his muscles moving angrily under the light wool of his suit, made her ache with renewed desire.

And more than that. Pulling the rough towelling tightly around her to mask the physical evidence of her response, Sasha knew that something had happened in the hours since Dirk had tucked her into his bed like a sick child and left her to sleep. Something irrevocable. She had fallen in love.

All night, she had lain between sheets where he had lain before her, breathing his soft, warm scent. All night she had been steeped in his invisible presence, absorbing the knowledge of him into every part of her.

Until she had woken to the sound of his voice, and opened her eyes to see his stern face bending over her. And had known, with no shadow of doubt, that she had loved him since the moment in Madame Zara's tent, when their hands and minds had touched. And that their fates were inextricably entwined.

But Dirk was in no mood for tenderness. Sasha pushed her new knowledge aside and did her best to apply her mind to his problem. 'Is there no one else who could deal with it? You don't have a partner?'

'Only my secretary, now that Mandy's gone, and she wouldn't have bothered me if it was anything she could cope with. This is hardly routine. One of our biggest backers is threatening to pull out—heaven knows why. There's nothing else for it; I'll have to go up and talk him round. But we'll lose another day's filming. Oh, hell!'

Dirk pulled up a chair and flopped down dispiritedly, running his hands through his already dishevelled hair. 'I'm beginning to think this blasted project is jinxed. We're already so far over budget that it's going to have to be the success of the year to make a decent profit. And if I have to start raking around for new finance...'

'But couldn't Owen and Stew be getting on while you're away?' she suggested tentatively. 'Presumably you'll have to pay them, anyway, so you might as well make use of them.'

He shook his head impatiently. 'It would never work. Not without direction. Owen's a great cameraman and Stew's good at his job, but they're technicians, nothing more. Even background and pick-up shots need a spark of creativity behind them.'

The germ of an idea crept into Sasha's mind. A very interesting idea. If she dared... 'What about me?'

'You? But I thought you had decided——'

'I've changed my mind.'

Dirk looked at her in amusement. 'Fancy yourself as a director, do you? It's not as easy as it looks, Sasha. Although I suppose it might be worth a try...'

She watched as he jumped up and walked over to the window. 'It's so damned annoying!' he burst out in obvious frustration. 'From the look of the sky, this might be the only day of decent weather we get all week, and I'm going to have to spend it toadying to some pot-bellied businessman who wouldn't know a social injustice unless it bit him right in the expense account.'

He turned back to her abruptly, seemingly coming to a decision. 'Do you think you could do it, Sasha? You've got my shooting script—but stick to the easy stuff, OK? Background, fill-ins... Forget the interviews and so on. They'll have to wait until I get back.'

Now that he had taken up her offer, Sasha began to feel considerably less confident. What did she know about directing? She'd never even made a home movie. But Dirk seemed to have latched on to the idea with enthusiasm.

'It doesn't matter if it doesn't work out; it's only the film that would go to waste. Even if you just get a few shots...I'd be less inclined to ram the stupid idiot's lunch straight down his throat if I thought something was at least happening.'

'I'll try...' Then another aspect of the situation struck her. 'But what about Owen and Stew?'

'Oh, they know what they're doing. You just point them in the right direction and they'll do the rest.'

'No, that wasn't what I meant.' Stew's hostile face floated into her mind. 'I mean, will they work for me? I'm hardly an expert, after all.'

'Oh, Owen will do anything for a laugh. And as for Stew...' His thoughtful expression made Sasha realise that he hadn't been as blind to the friction between them as she had thought. 'I'll have a word with them both now; make it clear that you're temporarily the boss and I expect them to follow your direction. I'll pitch it good and strong, don't worry. Stew may be a pain, but he's got his eye on his bonus. He'll be all right.'

She had to turn away to hide a smile. He was playing right into her hands. If he knew what she had in mind... But he didn't. It was her one chance to persuade him. And, by the time he found out, it would be done.

Sasha stepped back to survey the scene, still almost aghast at her own audacity. So far, it had gone unbelievably well, but this last shot was crucial to what she was trying to achieve. 'What about the light?' She looked anxiously at Owen, who gave her a cheerful thumbs-up.

'Perfect, darling,' he called cheekily from his position at the camera. 'Dark enough for the fire-light to show up, but not so dark you can't see the expressions on the little beggars' faces. Stop worrying; you've got it taped. The boss won't know what's hit him.'

Too right, he wouldn't, Sasha thought privately, as she gave the signal to start filming. He'd probably go berserk . . . She turned her attention back to the group around the fire: children and adults clustered around an old man with a violin under his chin and a disgusting old pipe hanging permanently from the corner of his mouth.

The story he was telling was in Romany, and far too rapid for her to follow. But the general outline was clear enough. Without moving from his seat or removing the pipe from his mouth, the storyteller took each part in turn, punctuating the story with bursts of music on the violin. Somehow, as if by magic, his wrinkled old face managed to express the emotions of the gypsy lover and his beloved; of her angry father and the old witch who helped the lovers thwart him.

His listeners were rapt; the adults as well as the children, although Sasha knew that all but the youngest would have heard the story before. The old man told two more in quick succession, one in English, then swooped straight into a rousing tune on the fiddle. To Sasha's delight, a few and then more of his audience took it up, stamping into a riotous impromptu dance. This was far more than she could have hoped for. If only the light would hold out... But Owen was still filming. They'd catch some of it, at least.

She felt a burst of light-headed happiness. She'd done it. In the scenes she had shot, she had managed to capture on film some of the aspects of gypsy life that Dirk was so determined to ignore. And with her grandmother's help she had made the gypsies her allies, drawing them into the film as active participants instead of angry victims.

Dirk might not use it, of course, but at least they knew she had tried. And once he saw it . . . Perhaps her film would prove more eloquent that her words.

A movement caught her eyes. Owen was waving at her, mouthing something unintelligible. It was probably the light; the summer evening was rapidly drawing in. Sasha yawned and stretched out her arms in weary satisfaction. It had been a good——

One hand hit something very solid. Sasha swung round with a startled yelp, to find herself staring at a very masculine shirt-front. Her eye skipped apprehensively up, past the open collar and loosened tie, to the shadowed chin and stern mouth. Oh, no. Her stomach twisted itself into an anxious knot. She had to force herself to meet his eyes . . .

And found them smiling. 'Oh, Dirk!' Excitement and relief poured out of her in a jumbled stream of words. 'It's gone so well! I don't know if it's what you want, but you must look at it. You will look at it, won't you? Even if——'

'Even if you totally ignored all my instructions?' he supplied ironically. But his tone was one of resigned amusement, not anger, and Sasha could have sung with relief. 'I suppose I should have known better than to expect you to be content with pick-up shots. What did Owen and Stew have to say about all this?'

'Well, you'd told them I was the boss . . .' Her eyes sparkled with mischief.

'So I did. A brilliant piece of stage-management on your part. I hope,' he added drily, 'it wasn't you who arranged for my man to develop cold feet? I never did manage to work out what had sparked him off.'

'I'm afraid not. Although now I've got a taste for directing...' She looked up at him teasingly. 'Do you have a list of your backers? I might give one or two of them a ring.' Then she remembered the serious side of his visit to London. 'How did it go, then?'

'Oh, I talked him round. Eventually. Of course, if I'd been able to tell him that I'd got a brilliant new assistant director on my staff...' He ruffled her hair in an affectionate gesture that left Sasha's heart beating at twice the normal rate. 'Come on, boss-lady. Let's go and reassure your crew that they've still got a job.'

'I won't come in.'

Sasha looked up from rummaging in her handbag for the cottage-keys, not bothering to hide her disappointment. 'Are you sure? After all, you've forgiven me for hijacking your film, and you've run me home. I must owe you a coffee, at least.'

It was the first time all evening that they had been alone, and she wanted desperately just to be with him a little longer. Perhaps over coffee she would be able to shake off the nervous formality that had afflicted her in the drive back to the cottage and let him know how she really felt. How her feelings had changed. And then——

But Dirk shook his head. 'You don't owe me anything, Sasha. And it's not coffee I want from you. You know that.' His eyes smiled down on her from the summer darkness, warming her. And she felt the nervousness thaw and melt away.

Her voice was a whisper. 'It's not just coffee I'm offering, Dirk.'

She could feel the stillness which gripped him at her words, and the surge of desire which followed it, electrifying them both with its primitive power. He took a hesitant step forwards, closing the gap between them to no more than inches.

And stopped. 'No, Sasha.' She stared up at him in bewilderment, and with a sigh he gathered her into his arms. 'Listen to me, little gypsy,' he said softly. His breath stirred her hair with its warmth. 'It's too soon.'

'No——' But as she turned her face up towards him he smothered her protest with softly compelling lips.

'Trust me. I've already made one mistake with you, and I don't plan to make any more. I guessed right the other morning, didn't I? It would be your first time?'

'Yes.' Sasha made the admission reluctantly. 'But what difference——? I want you, Dirk.' Her face burned in the semi-darkness, but she felt no shame. It was true, after all. And somehow, under cover of the tiny porch, there was no room for anything but truth between them.

'And I want you. But I can wait. It's a very precious gift you're offering me, Sasha. And I want you to be sure.'

'I am sure.'

'Are you?' She felt his arms tighten around her. 'Then why did you clam up this evening whenever Stew mentioned Mandy? Oh, I know he was deliberately trying to needle you. But he was succeeding, wasn't he?'

'No...' But her face must have betrayed her. It was as if he had read her mind.

'Listen, Sasha.' His voice was gentle, but unmistakably firm. 'Mandy and I were never serious.' He must have felt her silent protest, because he pulled her still closer, muffling her face in his chest. 'Or at least, I never thought we were. If I was wrong, I'm sorry; if I hurt her, I'm sorry. But whatever the rights and wrongs of it, it's over. You have to believe that, Sasha.'

'I do...' So why did she sound so uncertain, even to herself? 'I just feel so guilty, Dirk. If she knew about—about us, she'd feel so betrayed...'

'Would she? Perhaps you should ask her.'

'Oh, Dirk—I couldn't.' How many times in the last few days had she told herself the same thing? But it was impossible... How could she ever find the words to cause such pain?

'I think you must.' He looked at her in silence for a moment. 'I want to take you to bed, Sasha.' The blunt words sent a shudder of anticipation snaking down her back. 'I want to make love to you. I want to look down and see your face...'

He shook his head as if to clear the vision, gripping her shoulders fiercely as he spoke. 'Oh, Sasha—I'm starting to want all kinds of things I thought I'd never want. But I'm not into three-somes. I think you should talk to Mandy; tell her the truth. It's not your fault this happened. It's not anyone's fault. But until you believe that, she'll be standing between us like a ghost.'

There was a long silence. 'I suppose you're right,' Sasha said at last.

'I know I'm right.' He released her suddenly, almost pushing her away. 'Now, for pete's sake, find those keys before I run out of honourable intentions.' He watched silently as she found the keys and opened the door. His lips brushed hers and for a moment he seemed to hesitate. Then he swung abruptly away. 'I must be mad,' she heard him mutter, half to himself. 'Goodnight, little gypsy.'

'Goodnight, Dirk,' she whispered, and shut the door. But it wasn't until much later that she heard the car drive away.

Sasha floated through the next day on a cushion of happiness. He cared about her, that much was plain. And he had come so close to making some kind of declaration... But somehow, as the hours passed, the glow began to fade.

He treated her with a friendly intimacy that, she knew, convinced Owen and Stew that they were already lovers; but it went no further in private than it did outside. And to her disappointment he didn't even seem particularly curious about the footage she had shot during his absence.

'Don't get carried away, Sasha,' he had cut in when she tried to share her enthusiasm. 'Just because it felt good doesn't mean it'll come over; and

even if it does, it may not be right for *Travellers*.
If they're good, the pictures will speak for
themselves.'

But she knew from his voice that he had already
discounted the possibility. Well, perhaps he would
be surprised . . . But somehow, after his rebuff, she
couldn't recapture her feeling of confident triumph.

That night, and the next, sleep eluded her as she
stared into the darkness, playing and replaying his
words until they lost all meaning. The passion which
had showed itself so briefly began to seem as in-
substantial as a dream. If only they could talk . . .
But he seemed to go out of his way to avoid them
being alone.

And then there was Mandy. Contacting her had
proved more difficult than Sasha had expected.
Every time she dialled the number the other girl
had given her, the distant ringing went un-
answered. In desperation, she had even tried
phoning early in the morning and late at night, but
the result was the same. Mandy was simply never
at home.

And now time was running out. Tomorrow the
stalls and rides would be packed away and the long
caravan of lorries and trailers would move off to
their next stopping place. And Dirk would return
to London. Sasha knew that she didn't want him
to leave without something settled between them.

As she urged her van into life and set out for the
morning's rendezvous, she looked at the white envelope propped up on the dashboard. And yawned.
Composing it had taken her until the small hours
of the morning, but as she finally gummed down

the envelope and inked in Mandy's address, she had felt a new sense of freedom. At lunchtime, she would post it. And then perhaps they could move on.

She arrived at the fairground to find the place in turmoil. Although business was continuing, some of the bigger rides were already being dismantled and there was a general feeling of unrest permeating the place. Even the children looked nervous, hanging back and watching with wide, startled-deer eyes instead of pestering for sweets and pennies.

She hurried over to where the others were standing. 'What's happening, Dirk?'

'I don't know—we only just got here ourselves. Could we have got the date wrong? It looks like they're winding the place up.'

Sasha shook her head. 'Today's the final day, and I can't remember a time when the fair packed up early. Normally the last day's one of the best.' As a child, it had always been her favourite, in spite of the fact that it meant her grandmother was leaving. It had its own special atmosphere of celebration, for stall-holders and customers alike. 'Do you want me to go and find out what's happening?'

'If you could.' Dirk turned to the others. 'In the meantime, we'd better get moving. I want some shots of the stuff coming down—especially the Big Wheel. Sasha, that's where we'll be when you get back.'

Sasha nodded and turned away, making her way across the fairground to Madame Zara's booth.

'Hello, Gran.' The old lady was sitting behind a cloth-covered table, dressed in the full regalia of her calling. She was eating a sandwich. On the table lay a further plateful of sandwiches, a pack of cards and a crystal ball on a stand. Sasha smiled at the contrast and kissed her fragile cheek. 'How's things?'

'Better for me than for you, seemingly.' Sasha felt the sharp black eyes flicker over her face, taking in the circles under her eyes and the lack of colour in her cheeks. 'There's something bothering you, my girl. He been upsetting you, this Gorgio? Men, they're trouble right enough.' She burst into cackling laughter. 'But we wouldn't do without them. More fool us. So what's he been up to then, your King of Swords?'

The nickname, as always, gave Sasha a *frisson* of disquiet. Somehow she had never got round to telling the old lady about the 'coincidence' of Dirk's company name, as if to tell her would mean admitting that it was more than just coincidence. 'Nothing, Gran; he's fine. But what's going on round here? Why are they packing up early? Is something wrong?'

To her surprise, her grandmother glanced back over her shoulder and made a sign with her fingers to ward off evil. 'Had you not heard, *kushti*? Betty's man died in the hospital the other night. The fair's shutting down early for the funeral.'

For a moment Sasha was confused; then she remembered the gypsy superstition that to speak the name of a dead person was to risk calling back their *mulo* to haunt you. Of course, Dan Smith. She felt a pang of guilt as she realised that she had almost completely forgotten his involvement in the accident. The overriding relief at Dirk and Mandy's safety had wiped it from her mind.

'Oh—I'm sorry. I hadn't heard. When's it to be, the funeral?'

'This afternoon. It'll be a proper do as well; Betty's lot are real Romany.' She spoke with an almost gloating satisfaction that half shocked, half amused her granddaughter. The gypsies loved the drama of a funeral. 'And then they'll fire the trailer tomorrow morning to help him on his way. Will you be coming to follow the coffin, *kushti*?'

'If you think I'd be welcome,' Sasha said hesitantly. 'It sounds silly, but I feel I was involved somehow. I even feel a bit guilty—that I saw it and didn't save him. I think I'd like to come, if his family wouldn't mind.'

'Of course they won't, *kushti*. You come to the trailer first, if you're coming. We can walk up the road together.'

'I'll be there.' She gave the old lady a quick hug, realising guiltily how little time she had spent with her over the past week. Normally she spent most of her free time at the fair, but this year Dirk had taken priority... She was suddenly painfully aware that her grandmother couldn't go on for ever; that one year the fair would come to Horley and there would be a stranger in Madame Zara's tent.

The old lady gently disengaged herself from the embrace, looking at Sasha in concern. 'So tell me then, *kushti*. You're not happy.'

Sasha sat down and picked up a sandwich. 'Not unhappy, Gran. Just—unsettled.'

'Shall I be laying the cards again? To see how they come out?'

'No!' That was the last thing she wanted.

Her grandmother snorted in disgust. 'What are you—a Gorgio, to fear my *dukkering*? You're as bad as your mother with such silliness. And you have the gift yourself, girl; no good will come of denying it. There's a Romany and a Gorgio at war in your head, Sasha, but you're letting the Gorgio win. That's not right.'

She reached forward with sudden urgency and grasped Sasha's hand. 'You're your mother's daughter, *kushti*. You never did much favour your Da, even in looks. You're Romany more than you're Gorgio; inside where it matters. Don't let him make you forget it, this man. Or you'll not be happy. Your mother was so keen to be Gorgio, to please your Da, she ended up half alive. And it killed her in the end.'

'I know, Gran. But I'd never let that happen to me.' She felt a pang of disquiet as she made the confident pronouncement. If Dirk's feelings were serious... Could she really be so sure? She would never willingly give up the remnants of her gypsy background, but how long would she be able to resist the logic of his arguments; the gradual frustration of having her own experience contradicted and disbelieved?

'Then let me be, girl. I want to see...'

Sasha realised that her grandmother's gaze was fixed on the crystal in front of her, staring with absorbed concentration into its translucent depths.

'There is a woman stands between you...' Sasha had to fight back the impulse to run, to refuse to listen. The old lady was right; this was part of her heritage. Not something to fear. 'A fair-haired woman, *kushti*. Does that mean anything to you?'

'Yes.' The word came out as a whisper, and she cleared her throat nervously. She could feel her own fear like a cold hand on the back of her neck, trailing a chill finger down her spine. It was more than just the apprehension that her grandmother's gift always produced. Sasha realised she was terrified of what the old woman was going to say.

'She has been unhappy, but now that time is ending. She wears no ring, but one waits for her in the future.' The old voice caught suddenly, and she looked up at Sasha in concern. 'And *kushti*, this woman. She's pregnant. She's going to have a child.'

Her words flashed past Sasha's defences, burning themselves on her consciousness like lightning scars. It wasn't even a surprise, she realised drearily; she had seen it herself, in that brief glimpse as Mandy was leaving. A vision of future happiness... But if Mandy was already pregnant, it could only mean one thing. It was Dirk's child.

She could hear Mandy's voice echoing in her head. 'No goodbyes or anything. That was weeks ago.' How many weeks? However scatterbrained Mandy might be, she was bound to realise soon that something was wrong. Sasha felt cold with

relief as she remembered the letter on the dashboard of the van. If she had posted it . . .

'*Kushti*, are you all right?'

Sasha nodded blindly, realising for the first time
that her cheeks were wet with tears.

'You know her, then, this woman?'

'Yes.' Sasha hesitated, but the urge to confide
was strong. 'She's was Dirk's assistant when he
came here. And before that, they were lovers.'

The bald facts lay like rocks between them, cold
and hard. 'So you think it is his child?' Her grandmother frowned. 'No, girl, I don't believe it. I met
him; I read his hand. Your Gorgio is not a man to
desert his own child.'

Sasha shook her head. 'But, Gran—he doesn't
know. I don't even know if Mandy knows yet. And
when he does...' Her voice trailed hopelessly away.

The old lady looked troubled. 'They'll be
romered, you think, then?'

'Yes.' Sasha's voice was no more than a whisper.
Her grandmother was right. Dirk's sense of duty
would never allow him to turn his back on a woman
who was carrying his child, however little marriage
had figured in his plans.

'Then you must forget him, *kushti*.' The old
gypsy's cracked voice was sorrowful but firm. 'I'm
sorry for you, girl; and I'm sorry that I did what
I did to further it. But you must do what is right.'

'But I love him . . .' It was a cry of animal pain.

'I know it, Sasha. And the man loves you; it spills
from his eyes when he looks at you. But he will be

strong, and so must you.' The old woman paused, her back ramrod straight, like a judge about to pass sentence. Sasha could feel the compassion behind the inflexible purpose of her words.

'If this be true, you must not see him again, *kushti*. It would not be right.'

CHAPTER TEN

'But, Dirk, you can't possibly!' Sasha stared at him in horror, the other nightmare momentarily eclipsed by what he was suggesting. 'You'd get lynched for even suggesting it—and I don't think I'd blame them.'

'That's why I want you to suggest it. Look at the way they responded to you the day I was away. That dance—that was an amazing sequence, Sasha. They trust you. If you ask them, I'm sure they would agree.'

'No! No way, Dirk. It's a funeral, for goodness' sake, not a public spectacle. You can't possibly intrude at a time like that.'

'I wouldn't be intruding,' he pointed out calmly. 'Be reasonable, Sasha—you know how I'd handle it. It would all be done from a distance; no close-ups. They'd hardly know we were there. You ought to be pleased—you wanted me to get over that the gypsies are a real community with their own beliefs, their own customs. What better way to show it than this?'

'Oh, yes—that's right.' Sasha felt her general anger turn to a more personal bitterness at his calculated appeal. 'Now you want to talk me round, my ideas are all wonderful. Never mind that up to now you've shown about as much interest in them as you would in a re-make of *Alice in Wonderland*.'

'That's not true, Sasha. I just didn't want——'

'Don't try to kid me, Dirk. You want to film a private funeral and you want me to fix it for you. Well, I won't do it. What are you, some kind of ghoul?'

'You know what I am, Sasha.' His voice had a harsh edge to it now that he couldn't restrain. 'I make films. And I need these shots—not just the funeral but the *yagging* or whatever it was you called it as well. When they fire the trailer. It's a chance in a million that something like this should happen, and I won't pass it up.'

'The *yagging*? Now I know you're out of your mind.' Sasha took a step back, as if his lunacy might take a violent turn. 'That's just family, Dirk. Immediate family. It's a very private thing. A leave taking...'

'Sasha, I know that. Of course it's an emotional minefield—that's why it would be such a powerful scene. And I promise they wouldn't even see us. All I want is a shot of the flames leaping up against the darkness——'

'It happens at dawn,' she cut in flatly. 'That way the *mulo* has a whole day to travel before nightfall.'

'Against the dawn, then. You must see, Sasha. Think what a closing sequence it would make; the emotional charge it would leave. It would make the film unforgettable. The symbolism——'

'Damn the symbolism, Dirk! These are real people! A man is dead and you want me to ask his wife if she minds a camera peering over her shoulder while she says goodbye.'

'Hardly peering over her shoulder. We'd be the other side of the field.'

She could still hardly believe he was serious. 'You'd have to be the other side of the country before I'd take any part in it. And I mean that, Dirk. So forget it.'

As if he realised that she wasn't going to back down, Dirk shrugged. 'I want that film, Sasha. If you won't help, I'll ask for permission myself—and if I don't get it, I'll film anyway. But it would be better all round if you'd have a word with the family. That way, no one needs to get upset.'

'Upset?' The word was so inadequate that she almost laughed. 'You turn up anywhere near the *yagging* with that camera and you'll see how upset they are.' She waved towards the camera crew, who were watching the altercation with interest. 'I hope you're paying these two danger money. When gypsies get upset, they don't write letters to *The Times*, you know. They'll tear you apart.'

Owen and Stew looked at each other, and Sasha realised that this was an aspect of the situation that hadn't occurred to them. 'Have you seen old Dan's two boys?' she went on, guessing that her best chance of success was to play on their fears. 'They took that lorry half to pieces trying to get their Dad out. And they won't be alone. One hint of what you're planning, and you'll have every man between fourteen and sixty out for your blood.'

'Then couldn't you have a word, like?' Owen's voice was troubled, and Dirk knew she was winning. Even Dirk Kendrick couldn't make a film without someone to hold the camera.

'I told you—no way. If you want to stay in one piece, I suggest you persuade your boss to go and fire a hay-rick somewhere and film that instead. You only get sent to prison for that—not hospital.'

'Sasha, you're blowing this out of all proportion——'

'And so will Dan's wife and sons. Goodbye, Dirk.' She held out her hand in a formal gesture of farewell. 'I'll be going to the funeral—but as a guest, not a vampire.'

His hand closed on hers, and for a moment she thought he wasn't going to let her go. 'Please, Dirk,' she said quietly, 'think about it. This time you're wrong; and I'd hate you to find out the hard way.' The contact seemed to drain her anger. All that was left was an aching awareness of his closeness. When he released her, the sense of loss was like a physical pain.

Sasha turned and forced herself to walk away. Behind her, she heard a nasal voice raised in protest, and smiled bitterly. Stew was no war-zone correspondent. It would take more than artistic integrity to persuade him to risk his neck.

But her sense of satisfaction soon died. Without her anger to sustain her, the thoughts she had been suppressing came flooding back. 'You must forget him, *kushti*.' Her grandmother's words mobbed her unmercifully, like black birds of prey.

'Oh, let her be wrong,' she prayed silently as she set off across the field towards her cottage. 'Please, please let her be wrong.'

* * *

The funeral moved Sasha more than she had expected, with its strange mixture of the familiar and the totally alien. On to the quiet beauty of the English prayer-book ritual, in the mellow Cotswold stone of the Horley parish church, had been grafted something more like the funeral of some pagan chieftain.

In the normally silent churchyard, women wailed their grief with a complete lack of English reserve. And instead of the neat circular wreaths that adorned the other graves, the coffin was piled with intricate floral sculptures—chairs and tables; a dog and a television. All the comforts that old Dan had enjoyed in life were there, to join him in death. Even his lorry followed him, its number-plate faithfully reproduced with tiny blooms.

It was like something from another world. And yet the contrasts only underlined the inner meaning of the ceremony—the point at which the cultures met. Like two languages expressing the same thought, the Romany extravagance and the Gorgio restraint combined to form something that touched Sasha deeply. And, if the tears that she wept were not all for Dan Smith, she had the feeling he wouldn't have minded.

She left the church feeling stronger and somehow at peace. Only to have her illusions shattered. Before she had gone fifty yards down the road, Dirk's van emerged from the lane behind the church and swept past her, heading back in the direction of the Feathers. He had filmed the funeral, after all—which meant he was probably planning to invade the *yagging*, too. Somehow she had never quite believed he would be so callous.

Sasha felt something harden inside her. Swayed by her own feelings, she had let herself forget his ruthlessness. But this time he had gone too far. And it was up to her to stop him.

'Hello there, girl.' As Sasha walked into the Feathers, Owen's beery voice sounded almost in her ear and an arm snaked around her waist. 'Coming down to the bar, are you? We're having a bit of a drink, like, to celebrate our last night here.'

Sasha guessed that the 'bit of a drink' had already started as far as Owen was concerned. Well, so much the better. If Dirk was planning to film the *yagging*, she wanted to know all about it. The more talkative they were, the better. She let the big Welshman lead her into the bar.

'Hello, Stew.' Sasha ordered an orange juice and then joined Owen and Stew at their table. 'Where's Dirk, then?'

Stew didn't even look up, staring morosely at a soft drink in front of him. It was left to Owen to answer. 'Oh, he'll be down in a minute, girl, don't you worry. And don't mind Mr Cheerful here—he picked the short straw and he's driving tonight. Strictly forbidden to touch the demon drink.'

'Driving? Where to?' For a moment Sasha was confused. Surely they wouldn't be leaving already? But then Stew butted in and solved the mystery.

'You stupid old fool, Owen—keep your mouth shut. It's supposed to be a secret, remember?'

'Oh, the *yagging*.' She saw by their faces that she was right. 'Don't worry, Owen, I knew about that. Or at least, I guessed.'

'And you don't mind, like?'

Well, that confirmed that. Sasha shrugged in what she hoped was a dismissive manner. 'There's not much I can do to stop him. But I'm surprised you two are going along with it. I still think it's risky. Are you getting a bonus?'

Owen looked shamefaced. 'A whopping big one, to be honest with you, love. And he says he's had a word with them, like, to make it all right.'

Privately, Sasha doubted that the 'word', if it had existed at all, had covered anything except the actual funeral. It was inconceivable that the gypsies would have given permission to film one of their most private rituals. But she said nothing. She couldn't hope to compete with Dirk in persuasive power, especially when his arguments were backed by hard currency. She would have to think of another plan.

'So what's the set-up? I must say, you were discreet this afternoon at the funeral. I wouldn't have known you were there if I hadn't seen you leaving.' She kept her voice deliberately light, and felt slightly ashamed at the ease with which the burly man fell for it.

'Yes—he was very hot on that, the boss. Said we had to pretend it was one of these nature films we were making, and if we showed our noses we'd scare them away.' He groaned, and stretched out his arms. 'I spent half the afternoon doubled-up behind a hedge, and now I've got to spend half the night sleeping in that bloody van, so's we don't disturb

them by setting the stuff up tomorrow morning.
I'm getting too old for this game.'

'You're actually sleeping out? In the van?' Sasha
heard herself squeak with amazement at this fresh
evidence of Dirk's total determination. Inside she
quailed. Opposing him was more like taking on a
force of nature than fighting a mere mortal.

'That's right, girl. Come closing time and we'll
be off on our holidays. She's all packed up and
ready to go: sleeping-bags, cameras, bottle of
whisky—the lot.'

It was like a gift from heaven—a sign that even
forces of nature could be beaten. Suddenly, she
knew exactly what to do. 'You didn't notice a purse
lying around when you packed the van, did you?
Her heart was beating so loudly, it seemed impossible that the others couldn't hear it. 'I think I must
have dropped it yesterday.'

He shook his head. 'No, sorry. Though I can't
say I would have noticed, necessarily. There's a lot
of clutter.'

'Have you got the keys?' Sasha stood up and held
out her hand expectantly. 'I think I'll just go and
have a look.'

Owen looked taken aback. 'You'll never find it
in this light, girl. I'll have a look round tomorrow
for you.'

'No, that's OK. I think I know where it might
be.' Just give me the keys, she willed.

To her relief, it worked. Sasha walked casually
out of the bar, then flew out to the car park to find
the van. She unlocked the back doors and in-
spected the contents. It was all there. Cameras,

sound equipment—everything needed to make a film. And she had the keys.

Moments later, she was in the driver's seat, her fingers fumbling in her eagerness to start. She dropped the keys and bent down, cursing, to pick them up. But at last the engine sprang to life. She swung the van around the courtyard, heading for the exit. But when she got there it was blocked.

Not by the gate. But by a tall figure with a familiar face. And in the glare of the headlights that face was the grimmest she had ever seen.

Sasha.' He shook his head helplessly. 'I didn't mean
it to happen like this. I didn't want you to be upset.
I thought—— Oh, hell, Sasha, why do we do this
to each other? Why do we always end up fighting?'

He reached out a hand to wipe a tear from her
cheek. 'Sasha...' There was a moment of un-
bearable tension that seemed to stretch into an
eternity. And then they were in each other's arms,
and he was kissing her with a fierce passion that
answered her own need, overwhelming them both.

He drew hungrily on her lips, moulding her body
against him with his strong hands; and she responded, clinging to him as if their flesh could
merge—her softness with his taut strength.

'Oh, Sasha.' His open mouth caressed her as he
spoke, tasting, nuzzling at her lips and face, the
words themselves a caress that set her skin on fire.
'Oh, how I've wanted this. Every time I looked at
you... You don't know what you do to me, Sasha,
with those dark gypsy eyes of yours.' He kissed her
again, his words extinguished by his overriding
need.

And then she remembered. Pulling back was the
hardest thing she ever did, an almost imperceptible
movement in the prison of his arms. But it was
enough. She saw his eyes grow suddenly wary.
'Dirk, I——'

'What is it, Sasha?' His voice hardened and there
was a distance in his caress, as if he knew what was
coming. 'Is it more important than this?' His arms
loosened to let her pull away.

All she wanted was to say 'no', and abandon
herself to their passion. But something forced her

to go on, every word stabbing her heart with pain. 'I can't, Dirk. I——' I have to know if Mandy is carrying your child... But she couldn't say that. 'I'm still not sure, Dirk. I need more time.'

His hands were on her shoulders and Sasha could feel the tension in them. 'Your body is sure.' He pulled her closer, and his hand went to her breast. 'I want you, Sasha. And you want me. I can't wait any longer. Don't run away from me again.'

'I have to, Dirk. I—I can't explain. Not now. But we have to wait——'

'What is this, Sasha?' His eyes narrowed. 'It's Mandy, isn't it? You're still worried about Mandy.'

Her silence was admission enough. With a gesture of angry frustration, he pushed her away. 'Oh, Sasha—why are you tormenting yourself like this about something that ended months before we ever met? All it would take is one phone call...'

'I couldn't get through,' she said slowly, for something to say. But her mind was already spinning giddily off after that one crucial word. 'Months? What do you mean, months?'

He looked at her oddly. 'It's a fairly common word, Sasha. A division of the calendar into twelve parts——'

'No, idiot.' She could feel the hope bubbling inside her and fought to keep it back. 'You said it had been over for months. Is that true?'

'Of course it's true. What are you jabbering about, for heaven's sake? She joined me in April; April Fool's day, to be exact.' He shook his head impatiently. 'What possible significance——?'

All the significance in the world... Almost two and a half months. Not even Mandy could be two and a half months pregnant and not know it. Her grandmother had been wrong.

'You were right, Dirk.' She reached out and looped her arms round his waist. 'It isn't important.' Her hands gently circled his back, tugging his shirt free of his belt and slipping beneath it to glory in the sensation of skin on skin. For a moment, she thought he would reject her, but she felt his muscles tighten beneath her hand as he pulled her closer; and closer still, until she could hardly breathe.

'No more running, then, little gypsy?' His voice was fierce, but his eyes creased with tenderness.

'No more running.'

'Then come here.'

He led her over to the bed and sat down, pulling her towards him so that she stood between his knees. 'I want to see you, Sasha.'

She could feel her hands trembling as she undid the buttons of her blouse. There seemed to be more than she remembered... But at last, the demure cotton hung open, exposing the pale skin beneath.

'Take it off, Sasha.' His voice caressed her. 'I want you naked. And let down your hair.' His eyes never left her body as he started to unbutton his own shirt.

She shrugged the blouse from her shoulders, letting it fall to the floor, then reached behind her back to unhook her bra. As her breasts fell free of its lacy restraint, she tugged the band from her hair.

It fell like a shining black veil across the whiteness she had uncovered.

Dirk groaned and pulled her forward, winding his arms around her waist and burying his face in her soft flesh. 'You frighten me, little gypsy.' His hands caressed her, moving with restless hunger across her burning skin, tracing the swell of her hips, the curve of her thighs. 'You make me want so much. I want to hold you; I want to crush you in my arms and never let you go. I want to possess you... And you're so beautiful.'

His control broke and he tugged feverishly at the zip of her skirt, forcing it down. Sasha heard the fabric tear, but the sound was in another world. She kicked its soft folds away from her feet, knowing only that she wanted him and that the time was very near.

At last, she stood naked before him. He slipped off his jeans and pulled her down, rolling as she fell so that she ended beneath him, trapped in the cage of his body.

'Don't be afraid, little gypsy.' But there was no room for fear. His flesh nudged hers and she could feel a dampness between her own thighs. And a yearning... And then the hardness of him, pressing, invading.

There was a moment's pain, and then she was filled with him, and their bodies were moving together in an escalating spiral of passion that swept her beyond pain, beyond consciousness, beyond anything except the unimaginable pleasure of that fulfilment. He gasped her name, and she heard herself cry out in response.

And then she was falling, falling into darkness. And all she could hear was his voice, whispering. 'Oh, Sasha. Oh, my darling Sasha. Oh, my love.'

She lay in the semi-darkness, her head pillowed on Dirk's stomach, feeling it rise and fall with the rhythmic swell of his breath. Her fingers idly explored the line of crisp dark hairs that ran down from his chest. There was a sense of wonder about everything, as if together they had cast a spell which still permeated the atmosphere, drugging them with its enchantment.

'I like this,' she said absently, at last. 'Lying here with you breathing like this.'

'That's good.' Dirk shifted under her, propping himself on one elbow to look down at her in affectionate amusement. 'It bodes well for the future, that you like me breathing. I'd hate to have to give it up.' His voice changed in intensity. 'We do have a future, don't we, Sasha? When I go back to London, I want you to come with me.'

'Mmm.' She murmured her agreement to the honey-coloured skin beneath her cheek, flickering a tongue to taste its salty dampness. A warm glow of happiness began to swell and spread inside her. 'Just try to stop me, that's all. If you think you're editing *Travellers* without my help...'

He chuckled, and she felt the ripples of his laughter like waves caressing her. 'You'll make me seasick,' she scolded, tweaking a single hair with her teeth as a punishment and laughing herself when he yelped. 'My grandmother said this would be a stormy relationship.'

'That's not all she was right about. Look—no, don't move. Just turn your head—carefully.' Mystified, she obeyed his instructions. 'Look at your hair.'

The fine strands were spread fanlike across his body and thighs, their dark network reaching almost to his knees. '"A net to capture your heart's desire," she said, didn't she? And look what it's caught.'

'Egotist.' She ran her hand down the black river, stroking him with its silky fullness. 'Perhaps I'd better start trawling,' she teased mischievously. 'It would be a shame to let a catch like that get away.' His body stirred under her hand, and a new flood of desire poured through her, washing away the languor.

She heard him catch his breath in pleasure. 'Come here, wanton.' He pulled her up beside him, trapping her wrists in his hands. 'Or you may get more than you bargained for.' With infinite delicacy his warm mouth caressed the peak of each pale breast, coaxing them to rosy firmness. Sasha gasped, then abandoned herself to the pleasure as his lips moved down her body, lighting a fire of erotic sensation in their wake.

'This one's for you, little gypsy,' he murmured. 'And I want it to last a long, long time.'

It was dark when she woke, and she was cold. Cold right through. And something was wrong. But, with the strangeness of the room and her own feelings, it took her a few drowsy minutes to work out what it was.

She was alone. Dirk had been with her, in this bed, and they had made love. If she had doubted the memories that flooded back into her half-waking mind, her own flesh bore the proof: naked, tender and chilled to stiffness by the cool night air. His hard body had driven her so far into pleasure that it was almost pain; plundering her, savaging her, relentless in his need and in his giving. And she would never be the same.

Sasha knew only that she had never dreamt that such pleasure could exist; and that he had awakened her. He had changed her utterly. She knew what the old cliché meant now; and the truth of it. She was a woman at last. He had transformed her.

Wonderingly, she ran her hands over her naked-ness, feeling her new woman's body. As if she had opened out, her flesh felt softer, more yielding. She was a bud that had burst into bloom. Her breasts felt full and voluptuous as she touched them, and she found herself remembering... Remembering how his hands had moulded their softness, how his mouth had teased them into peaks of ice and fire.

And how he had fallen asleep half sprawled across her, his face buried in the dark mass of her hair. She had drifted slowly after him, savouring the extra moments of consciousness before ex-haustion claimed her, watching him greedily. In sleep, his face had lost it sternness, giving him a boyish, innocent look. She had stored the picture away, like a mental photograph. It would be some-thing she would always remember.

But the original had gone. Sasha forced herself awake and sat up, pulling the discarded duvet from the floor to wrap around her shoulders and quell the shivering which racked her. 'Dirk?' But she expected no answer. The silence which surrounded her was too complete. She was alone. And, when the first grey tendril of light came creeping into the room, she realised why.

Dragging the duvet behind her, Sasha ran over to the window and looked out over the fields behind the inn. As her eyes became accustomed to the dimness, she could make out the shapes of buildings and hedges; and the dark clump of trees that marked the gypsy encampment.

For a while there was nothing else. Then a flicker, so faint at first that she thought her eyes had invented it. And another and another, until the red glow of the burning trailer blazed clearly against the darkness of the trees and the grey smoke twirled and twisted into the grey dawn sky. Dan Smith's *mulo* was leaving on his last journey. And Dirk Kendrick was out there, filming it, as if their passion had never been.

The flames reached their zenith, flared and danced and died quickly. But the glow of the embers lived on. Not until the last trace of red was quenched by the dawning daylight did Sasha move stiffly away from the window. It was over. He had won. And she had failed.

He had betrayed her. It had all been a sham, a trick to ensure her quiescence. He had used her, as he had used her all along. He had called her his love and then crept from her bed in the darkness to keep faith with his precious film.

He had even warned her, once, what he was like. Totally dedicated and completely ruthless... But, like a fool, she had heard the words and never listened to their meaning. Completely ruthless. And this was the man she had allowed herself to love.

She sat on the bed, the duvet huddled round her, wondering why she didn't cry. But her grief seemed to be locked into a ball of ice which twisted her stomach into knots of pain and there was no relief through tears. For the first time she understood why the gypsies wailed their grief. She could have howled, screamed, cried out with the agony of it. But she did nothing. Just rocked back and forth as if she were a child again, and the anguish were a colic from eating too many unripe apples from the old tree.

She might have sat there for hours. But somewhere in another room a clock struck five, and the quavering notes penetrated her dream, stirring her to action. Of course. He would be back soon. If she didn't want to see him, she would have to act quickly.

Her first thought was for the door. Had he locked it? Dropping the duvet, she ran across in panic to check, but to her relief the key hung in the lock. And then she noticed something else—a scrap of white paper tied to the key-ring, fluttering in the draught from the cracks round the door.

She reached for it, and saw that there was writing on one side. Her heart started to beat faster and a small flame of hope started to melt the edges of the ice. A note. Had she misjudged him, after all? Perhaps something had happened to call him away.

Impatiently, she tugged the paper free of the key-ring.

The note consisted of three words, the firm, black lettering instantly recognisable as Dirk's.

'No more running.'

And that was all.

Sasha looked again at her watch, and back at the door, pleading for it to open and him to be there. It was almost twenty minutes since she had heard them arrive back at the inn, and still Dirk hadn't come.

Where was he? It had taken all her courage to stay, fighting the urge to escape before he could hurt her again. She had none left for this intolerable waiting. What could be more important to him than finishing what they had started the previous night? It was no use. She couldn't bear it. She decided to go down.

She heard his voice before she rounded the bend in the stairs and stopped, not wanting to interrupt if he wasn't alone. The words floated up to her and she listened impatiently.

'Yes, of course I'm pleased.' But he didn't sound pleased, she thought with detachment. He sounded worried, angry. 'But it's a big step to take, and I'm not sure you've considered all the consequences. I just don't think you should rush into something that will change your whole life without making sure——'

He stopped, as if listening, and Sasha realised in surprise that he must be on the phone. But what sort of person made phone calls at six o'clock in the morning? She wondered whether he would see her if she crept past to the dining-room; she didn't particularly want to eavesdrop on his entire conversation.

But Dirk was speaking again. 'Yes, I know you are,' he went on. 'But there are ways out of that. You don't have to go through with it unless you're certain that's what you want.' Another pause. 'Yes, yes—of course. If it is what you want, of course I'll be there at the church. I wouldn't desert you, Mandy, you know that.'

There was another long silence. Sasha felt herself sway and nearly fall, clutching the stair-rail for support. No wonder Dirk hadn't come straight to his room. There must have been a message waiting for him. She had thought nothing could be more important than what they had shared, but she had been wrong. And her grandmother had been right.

Afterwards, she could never remember how she got to the van, but she must have had the sense to go down the back stairs, because no one followed her. And for once the engine fired first time. As she turned out on to the silent high street, she hesitated momentarily, wondering whether she could risk a visit to the cottage. But she decided against it. It was the first place Dirk would look if he came after her. She had to be sure of her escape.

As she drove, she mentally reviewed her position. The little camper was stocked with food and a couple of changes of clothes. Her passport and spare cheque-book were stashed, as always, in the First-Aid box hidden down by the spare wheel. There was nothing else she needed; nothing that she couldn't do without. Except Dirk. And he belonged to Mandy, and their child.

It was as if her whole life had been a preparation for this to happen. As if she had always known... At the bottom of Pedlars Hill, she turned right towards freedom, settling her foot on the accelerator and driving blindly on.

Out of Horley. Away from Dirk. And into the bleakness of a future without love.

CHAPTER TWELVE

IT WAS a little bar in southern France, just like thousands of other little bars all over Europe. It was dark and not very clean, and a television flickered silently above the bar. But the food was good, and Sasha wasn't particularly bothered about the dirt. As she ate, her hand went down occasionally to check the presence of the bag she carried with her—the bag that contained her precious manuscript. After all these months, it had become a reflex action. The other patrons ignored her, drinking their red wine and playing some complicated card game with much gesticulation and heated argument.

She finished the hot soup, wiping the plate clean with a slice of crusty bread in the French way. At last, her fingers were beginning to thaw out. She flexed them experimentally, wondering whether she could afford a room for the night. January was a bad time of year to be sleeping in the van, and now it was snowing... A place like this wouldn't be expensive; she'd probably spend almost as much on the petrol to keep the heater going.

And she could do with a bath. She calculated that the kitty could just manage it. With luck, there would be money waiting for her at the post office in Toulouse. That series of articles she had sold; surely her agent must have been paid for them by now? And the rent from the cottage—the quarterly cheque had been well overdue last time she picked up her mail.

The *patron* cleared away her bowl and replaced it by a steaming plate of some kind of stew with beans in it. Sasha fell on it ravenously, washing it down with mouthfuls of the rough local wine which came included in the price of the meal. A feeling of well-being settled over her, and she decided that she would definitely stay the night. She was warm now... She sat back contentedly, the last glassful of wine in her hand, and mentally rehearsed what to say. She had been back in France less than a week, and it was still the Spanish words that sprang first to mind.

When the man came back to clear away, she stumbled through her request. Yes, he had a room. It was small, but it was cheap. And she could use the bath, but there would be *un supplément*—an extra charge. If *mademoiselle* would be so kind as to pay in advance... She paid up.

Above the bar in front of her, the television pictures flowed silently past. Sasha wondered idly why it was that they never turned the sound up in these places. Except for the football—and then you could hardly hear the commentary for the contributions of the audience. Adverts in particular looked even more inane without the sound. She watched a woman apparently swooning with pleasure as the result of eating a chocolate biscuit, and giggled out loud.

The card players turned to look at her, and she heard one of them mutter, *'Tzigane.'* Gypsy. Then they turned back to their game. Sasha fingered the room-key that lay in front of her, glad that she had already paid. If the *patron* had heard them... It wouldn't have been the first time she had been turned down for accommodation on the grounds of her gypsyish appearance. Still, no doubt she did look somewhat road-weary. It would be good to have a night in a real bed. Dismissing their prejudice from her mind, she turned her attention back to the screen.

The adverts were over, and some kind of film was showing. Sasha thought sleepily that she must have seen it before; there was something familiar about it. Perhaps she should go straight up and have that bath... But then a long shot showed what seemed to be gypsy encampment, and she sat forward with interest. The film cut to an old woman moving around in a cramped caravan interior. The woman's face was turned away from the camera, but Sasha felt a prickle of recognition in the back of her neck. It couldn't be... But it was. And then she realised.

She was watching *Travellers*.

'Please, please—the sound...' Sasha waved her arms frantically at the television, all her French deserting her in her panic. The *patron* looked at her suspiciously, then shrugged his lack of understanding and made as if to continue with his washing of glasses.

'Please—*s'il vous plaît, monsieur*...' She made twiddling gestures with her fingers. *'Le son...'* Did that mean sound, or was it something to do with wheat? She had to make him understand. *'C'est ma grandmère——'*

As the screen was at that moment showing two large and very male gypsies haggling over a piebald horse, Sasha's declaration that it was her grandmother served only to convince the *patron* that he was dealing with a lunatic. He shook his head and started to shuffle off towards the kitchen. But luckily one of the card players had caught her drift, and launched into a voluble stream of unintelligible explanation in which the word *'tzigane'* figured several times.

At last the penny dropped. All those present said 'Aaah!' to each other in varying degrees of enlightenment. A chair was ceremonially dragged forwards and the least decrepit of the card players clambered up to adjust the volume. Sasha was waved back to her seat as if she were the guest of honour at some star-studded matinée, and the *patron* shouted for his wife, who waddled out of the kitchen to join them. The card game was abandoned as all the participants gathered round with avid interest to watch the show.

The commentary was in English with French subtitles which her companions insisted on reading aloud for each other's benefit. But, even under such unpromising conditions, the film's power was unmistakable. And more than that... As she watched, Sasha gradually came to realise that it was subtly different from the early version Dirk had shown her at the Feathers. He had used the scenes she had shot and others that she didn't recognise, their optimism woven into the film's dark tapestry like a golden thread of hope.

Dirk had taken her suggestions and transformed them with his own vision, producing a film that said everything she had tried so haltingly to explain to him, without ever compromising its harsher message. It was a triumph. And when at last it ended, on a long, silent shot of Dan Smith's blazing caravan, Sasha was unashamedly in tears. He had been right. It was the perfect ending, and there was nothing intrusive about it. She should have known . . .

The credits rolled, and Sasha pushed back her chair. But to her surprise the others gestured her to stay. It wasn't finished. Patiently, she sat through adverts for coffee and washing powder, wondering what they could mean. She soon found out. After the break, an interview had been set up with the film's director. And Dirk and Mandy were smiling at her from the screen.

Seeing him again after so long was like a blow to the heart, but Sasha leaned forward eagerly, desperate for more. It was a frustrating experience. The interview was dubbed, not subtitled, and it was oddly disorientating to hear a stranger's voice issuing from that familiar mouth. And worse, she could understand very little of the rapid exchange of French. With the help of her unofficial translators, she gathered that the film had won some kind of award. It didn't surprise her. But she would rather have heard it from Dirk's lips.

But at least she could see him. That was something. And in some ways it was more than enough.

Dirk was thinner, his face more angular than ever. And, although he smiled in all the right places, his eyes were stern. Her heart went out to him. *Oh, Dirk*... The longing hadn't lessened over the months, she realised sadly. Time might be the great healer, but no healer could regenerate a lost limb. Or a lost heart. If only...

He was fiddling with something in his breast pocket, fingering it and sometimes almost pulling it into view before he realised what he was doing. It was probably the microphone—from her own filming experience, Sasha knew how irritating they could be. Whatever it was, he didn't seem able to leave it alone, and the unconscious gesture made him seem suddenly very real.

But it was his companion who was the revelation. If she had ever doubted the wisdom of leaving, Sasha knew now that she had done the right thing. Mandy seemed to glow with the inner radiance that was more than beauty. Sasha didn't need to look at her hand to see the rings which nestled there. Her friend was the very picture of a contented young wife.

Her pregnancy was obvious now and she looked utterly happy, like an expectant madonna. With a shock of recognition, Sasha realised that she was seeing again the picture she had glimpsed all those months ago, as Mandy was leaving. Except that, this time, the man's face wasn't in shadow... She counted off the time on her fingers and realised that the programme must have been recorded. By this time, the baby would have been born...

'Oh, Mandy,' she whispered at last, as the interview came to an end, 'please make him happy. Please...' It was all too much. Resting her head on the table in front of her, Sasha abandoned herself to her grief.

'*Ah, la pauvre petite!*' The wife of the *patron* thrust a large glass of brandy into Sasha's hand and made gestures that she should drink it up. Its fiery warmth made her cough and splutter, but the generosity of the gesture forced her to finish it, sipping slowly.

'I'm sorry——' she started in uncertain French.

But *madame* would have no apologies. But it was natural! A young woman so far from her family, and then to see them on the television. And the director, too, she knew him perhaps? An old friend? Ah, yes; she had thought as much. But why did Sasha not go back to England, since she missed them so? 'You are too independent, you young ones,' she scolded. 'All this travelling—and alone! Small wonder that you find yourself desolated. You should go back to your friends.'

By this time, the brandy had done its work, pulling a hazy screen between her and her grief. Sasha stood up carefully and announced that she was going to bed. It was a long leave-taking, with hands to be shaken and cheeks kissed. But at last she was standing alone in the little room her *francs* had bought for her, and she knew that *madame* was right. There was no longer any reason for running.

It was time to go home.

* * *

In the morning, her decision was still firm. It made
sense in a lot of ways, although the word 'home'
had a bitter emptiness about it. Where was home,
when her cottage was rented out to strangers and
when the only man she would ever care about was
married to another woman—and by this time, the
father of her child? But the book was almost finished, CTV were planning a second series of *Foresight*, and the van's health was becoming more
fragile by the day. And, however bleak the prospect,
it was the only home she had.

Sasha said goodbye to the *patron* and was re-
peatedly engulfed in *madame's* scented pillow of a
bosom by way of reward for her good sense. Now
that the decision was made, she was anxious to be
off. She spent that night in a lay-by south of
Limoges. Two days later, she was in England.

It was a strange homecoming. The van had
broken down just outside Chesley, and it had taken
her two hours to fix it, struggling in the snow. But
she had done it in the end, and her new-found skill
gave her the pleasure it always did.

So many things about her had changed during
her absence—so many things had had to change.
She had the curious feeling that the village would
have shrunk, the way places remembered from
childhood always seem smaller when revisited as an
adult.

But it was just the same. She crawled up Pedlars
Hill, the snow still falling thickly in the darkness.
How many years was it since she had seen the snow
so deep? At the top of the hill she stopped and
looked at her watch. It was later than she had

planned: half-past ten. It would be sensible to drive straight to the Feathers. But she wanted so much to see the cottage—and it would only be five minutes out of her way. She would just drive past it. Just to feel she was home.

It took her ten minutes longer than usual, but she made it. The cottage was still there, a light in the bedroom window, looking prettier than ever with its thatch covered with snow. And someone had repaired the gate, and mended the porch light ... Sasha slowed down to take a closer look at the changes.

And then the van stalled. A couple of abortive turns of the key convinced her that re-starting it was likely to be another two-hour job, and she was already wet through and cold. There was nothing else for it. She would have to call at the cottage and ask to use the phone.

She trudged her way up the path and rang the doorbell, noticing as she did so that the door had been treated to a fresh coat of paint. But they had kept the same colour. Sasha found herself approving of these unknown people; they showed sensitivity. It seemed she had left the cottage in good hands.

The door opened just as she was wondering how she should introduce herself. Should she tell them she owned the cottage? But no introductions were necessary. The man who stood on the threshold of her cottage, a towelling bathrobe wrapped loosely round him, was Dirk Kendrick.

Her first reaction was one of pure, unqualified joy. A cry from the heart. But it was overtaken almost before it could register by one of pain. How could he be so cruel as to bring his wife and child to her cottage? And to think she had been crediting him with sensitivity...

'Sasha.' He was staring at her as if he had seen a ghost. 'Sasha.'

'Hello, Dirk.' If she could just get through this without breaking down... 'This is a surprise.' She struggled to keep it light and friendly. *He mustn't know.*

'What——' His voice cracked, and his tongue flickered over his lips. 'What are you doing here?'

'As of this moment, freezing to death. I drove up here to look at the cottage and my van's conked out. I just want to use my—your—phone.'

He stepped back hurriedly, beckoning her inside. 'I'm sorry, come in. It's just such a shock——'

He didn't seem to be able to keep his eyes off her, looking at her with such hunger that Sasha felt her heart lurch. He feels it, too, she thought. It was a mistake to come. She walked quickly past him into the living-room. Six months away, and it was still there, a fire smouldering in the bracken, just waiting for the wind to freshen for it to leap out anew. She would have to take care they didn't meet again.

'Sasha...'

'Do you have the number of the Feathers? I'll get them to send a car round.' She felt instinctively that she had to stop him speaking. Once the words were said, the thing that was between them would take shape and form. The wind would fan the flames and they would be powerless to contain it.

'How's Mandy? And the baby? I haven't been totally out of touch, you know. I've heard all the news. And I saw *Travellers*, Dirk. It was brilliant.' She paused and smiled. 'And true.'

'Thanks to you. I owe you a lot, Sasha. Did you hear it won an award?' He walked to the table and picked up a telephone directory, then put it back down. Sasha realised that he was as nervous as she was herself. 'Mandy's fine. And the baby's due in March.' He looked at her again, with that hunger that frightened her. 'Sasha, you don't have to ring the Feathers. You can stay here.' He saw her face and added, 'There's a spare room.'

But, almost without wanting to, her mind was checking the sums. 'Oh, I don't think that would be a good idea, do you? And besides, I'd hate to put Mandy to any trouble.' She couldn't help the waspish emphasis; she was almost shaking with anger. All this time, she had believed him... But if the baby wasn't due until March, he must have been sleeping with Mandy only a short time before they met.

But he was staring at her in puzzlement. 'Mandy? What are you talking about, Sasha? She's not here.'

'Not here? Where is she, then?' If he had the gall to suggest that she stay, since his wife was away, Sasha felt she would kill him.

'At home, I expect.' His eyes captured hers and held them against her will. 'With her husband.'

'Oh——' Sasha felt the blood drain away from her face, and slumped down on the sofa behind her. 'What do you mean, Dirk?' she whispered. 'What about the baby?'

'Well, I expect it's there too, if Mandy is. It doesn't have much choice, at that age. What is this about Mandy, Sasha? Why did you think she'd be here?'

'I thought . . .' Her voice trailed away. Could she really have been so wrong? But she was afraid to let herself hope; afraid that she would just be crushed again.

'What did you think, Sasha? What made you bolt like that? I knew you'd be angry about me filming the *yagging*, but I told myself you wouldn't even wake up. And even if you did . . . I left you a note, Sasha. You should have waited.'

'I did. I was angry, but I read the note and I waited. But you didn't come. And then I heard you talking to Mandy, on the phone.' She fixed her mind on that one point of certainty. She had heard him, there was no doubt about that. He couldn't explain that away.

'And? Sasha, you're not making a lot of sense here. I know you always had a bee in your bonnet about Mandy, but you can't be telling me you ran away just because I talked to her on the phone?'

'No, I——' She took a deep breath and came straight out with it. 'I heard what you were saying, you see. About the baby. I know it's yours. And you said you'd marry her—I thought you had. What happened, Dirk? Did she meet someone else?'

He shook his head slowly, as if trying to jar something loose. 'Let's take this slowly, Sasha. Mandy married her new boss, Dave, about a month after you left. I didn't know anything about the baby until after the wedding, and it certainly isn't mine. And I never had the slightest intention of marrying Mandy, either before or after we split up. Does that clarify anything for you? Because I don't have the faintest idea what you're talking about.'

'But I saw you on television together . . . being interviewed. And that phone call—Dirk, I heard it. You can't just deny it ever happened.'

'Sasha, appearing on television with someone is hardly evidence of matrimony. Mandy was at the awards ceremony because one of Dave's travel films was shortlisted for an award. So, since she'd worked with me on *Travellers*, they interviewed us together, that's all. And as for the phone call, I wouldn't dream of denying it. But either we're talking about different conversations, or else you've been playing Chinese Whispers with what I said.'

'But I heard——'

'What did you hear? Sasha, when I got back that morning, I had no intention of doing anything but re-joining you in that bed as soon as possible, and making sure that you didn't leave it until I was forgiven. And believe me, I was looking forward to persuading you.'

Dirk walked across and sat beside her on the sofa. Sasha could feel his closeness like an electric charge—and she could feel him willing her to look at him. But she didn't dare. Not until she had heard the whole story.

'There was a message waiting for me at reception, from Mandy. To ring her urgently, whatever time I came in. I thought at the very least she'd had some sort of accident, so I phoned her. Only to find that she'd been high on champagne when she left the message and all she wanted was to tell me she was engaged to Dave and ask me to give her away at the wedding.' Dirk reached out and gently turned her face towards him. 'Her father died when she was small, you see, Sasha. So she had no one else.'

Sasha realised she had been holding her breath. She let it out in a long sigh of understanding. What he was saying was the truth; she could feel it. 'And you said you'd be there at the church—that you wouldn't let her down.'

'Something like that, I suppose. And you thought—— Hell, Sasha, didn't it occur to you to ask me? And however did you get the idea she was having my baby?'

'I don't know.' It all seemed so dim, now, like a memory of sickness. 'I can't remember what you said, exactly—but it was something about how it would change her life, and she didn't have to go through with it if she didn't want to. I thought she had told you she was pregnant and you wanted her to get rid of it.'

Dirk looked at her appalled. 'That was her engagement I was talking about. It all seemed so rushed—and you know what Mandy's like. She isn't fit to be let out without a keeper. She'd been mooning over me just a few days before and I had this terrible feeling that she was trying to prove something. Provoke a reaction. Egotistical of me, I know—and as it turned out, I was wrong. But I can't see how you could have jumped to such a stupid conclusion.'

'No.' How had she never realised how inconclusive the whole thing was? But she had been predisposed to believe it. 'It was Gran. That morning. She told me Mandy was pregnant. That's why I wouldn't—why I held back at first. Until you told me when you and Mandy split up, and then I thought it couldn't be true. But when I heard you on the phone, it just seemed to confirm everything.' She looked at him timidly, expecting his anger. 'I'm sorry, Dirk. But I was already upset about the *yagging*... And Gran's not often wrong.'

But to her surprise he just smiled. 'I don't suppose she was this time, either. I have a lot of respect for your Gran.'

'You mean Mandy *was* pregnant then? By her new boss?'

Dirk nodded. 'Only just, but it would fit in—I gather it was something of a whirlwind romance.' He smiled wryly. 'Like ours—but Dave had more sense than I did. He didn't waste time acting the gentleman. Or crawling round the countryside when he should have been in bed.'

'So Gran was right.'

'And your conclusions were wrong, Sasha.' His eyes were suddenly serious. 'I meant what I said in that note, little gypsy. No more running. If we hit problems, we'll sort them out.' He drew her towards him and held her close. 'Together.'

The nightmare was over. Sasha clung to him wordlessly, feeling the fears and miseries of the past months ebb away, leaving her light and floating. 'Together.' A great bubble of happiness seemed to be swelling inside her. It was going to be all right.

Dirk held her tightly for a moment, then drew back in concern. 'Sasha, you're frozen. And wet through. I'll run you a bath.'

He made as if to stand up, but she wouldn't let him go, her hands creeping into the warmth beneath his robe and her face nuzzling his chest. 'Couldn't we just go to bed?'

'Good lord, woman.' He curled his lip in mock distaste. 'You're like a drowned rat. If you think I'm letting a tatty little object like you into my bed——'

'Who said you were letting me into your bed? The last thing I heard, you were offering me the spare room.' She smiled up at him wickedly, her eyes dancing with fun.

'That was just to allay your maidenly fears. But I'm not prepared to go the whole way at this stage in our relationship. I may be letting you into my bed, but I'm not letting you out.' He grabbed her suddenly, heaving her up over his shoulder in a fireman's lift. 'You forget, I've got seven months of wasted time to make up. And so, I hope, have you.'

'Oh, not wasted exactly,' she said dreamily, as he carried her up the stairs. 'Ow!'

He threw her on to the bed. 'Get those disgusting clothes off. And while you're doing that, you can tell me what you've been doing all this time. And if I don't approve, I'm going to throw you back into the snow.'

'Well, there was Morrish. And Rico and Fernandez, and Batiste.' She undid the buttons of her shirt contemplatively. 'And Django, of course.'

He pounced on her vengefully, and she screamed, her eyes alight with excitement.

'I've been "off with the raggle-taggle gypsies-oh", Dirk.' She twisted round underneath him, pulling off her shirt and unzipping her wet jeans. 'I've been all over Spain and France. And I've written a book. It's almost finished. A novel, about the gypsies. And my agent's seen bits of it, and she thinks it's good. In fact, better than that. She thinks it might even sell!'

'That's marvellous, Sasha.' He kissed her, with lips that burnt like fire on her icy skin. 'You've changed, little one.'

'I know. Do you remember that first night when you took me out to dinner? You asked me who the real Sasha Dinwoodie was. I couldn't have told you then, I don't think. But now I know. Or at least, I'm beginning to find out.' She gave a complicated heave, trying to ease her damp-tightened jeans over her hips.

'That's good.' He watched her struggles with detached interest. 'Now you can start on Sasha Kendrick. Are you taking those off, or aren't you?'

'They're stuck.' Sasha Kendrick. 'Is that a proposal?'

'Let me at them.' With one pull, the wet denim was round her feet and she kicked it off on to the floor. 'Of course it's a proposal. If you think I'm letting you out of my sight until there's a ring safely on your finger... In fact, I'm thinking of asking if we could be married in handcuffs. Jewelled, of course.'

He flipped her over and dealt dexterously with the hook of her bra, then started to slide her panties slowly down her legs. Sasha lay on her stomach and stretched out, luxuriously passive, revelling in the sensation of his warm hands on her cold skin.

But her outstretched hand found something under the pillow. A little leather bag... It was somehow familiar. She pulled it out and stared at it in puzzlement. 'What's this, Dirk?'

'You ought to know, Madame Zara. Your grandmother made it.'

'Dirk! It's a calling bag! What on earth——?'

'I was desperate, Sasha. I tried everything: private investigators, everything. But you'd vanished from the face of the earth. I felt so helpless...' The anguish came through in his voice, and Sasha rolled over, reaching out instinctively to comfort him.

'It made me realise what a fool I'd been, to risk losing you... I wanted that scene so badly—I was convinced I was right.'

'You were right, Dirk.' She snuggled more closely into the curve of his body, basking in his warmth. 'It was the perfect ending.'

'But I should have talked to you, persuaded you. Nothing was worth that risk.' He touched her gently, as if he could hardly believe she was really there. 'I've changed too, Sasha. I'll never do that to you again.

'So, anyway, when I couldn't track you down, I traced your Gran. I thought she might know something. And I remembered what she said, that time she read my palm. About finding something for me—"Something precious, something lost". She made the charm for me.'

With a sudden flash of insight, Sasha remembered. 'That's what you were fiddling with, wasn't it, Dirk? On the interview on French TV. After *Travellers*. You were wearing it over your heart.'

'"Over my heart by day, and under my pillow by night".' He gestured towards the pillow. 'I told you I was desperate.'

He looked so embarrassed that she felt almost sorry for him. But his next words convinced her that the old Dirk Kendrick was still very much alive. 'Of course, I knew it would never work.' He grinned teasingly at her expression of outrage.

'What do you mean? I'm here, aren't I? Oh, don't tell me. It's just coincidence, right? I just happened to see you on French television and you just happened to be fiddling with it and I just happened to decide to come home, is that it?'

He nibbled gently on her ear, nuzzling her neck. 'That's it. These things happen.'

'And you just happened to be staying in my cottage?'

'Certainly not!' He turned his attention to her breasts. 'There was nothing accidental about that. That was my contribution—sheer logic. If you were going to turn up anywhere, it would be here. I just thought it might give coincidence a helping hand.'

'I see.' The warm softness of his mouth was stirring a dreamily liquid sensation in the pit of her stomach. 'And my van breaking down outside; that was coincidence as well?'

'Of course.'

She rolled away from him, dangling the little bag just out of reach. 'In that case, you won't mind if I look inside it... I've always wondered——'

'Oh, no, you don't.' Sasha gasped as Dirk's full weight came sprawling across her naked body and her wrist was gripped in a hand like steel. He grinned sheepishly. 'I may not be superstitious, but I'm not stupid. I'm not taking any chances. That particular coincidence is staying intact.'

Sasha felt the bubble of happiness burst inside her, flooding her with joy. 'Oh, Dirk. We'll make a proper Romany of you yet. I always did get the feeling that you could read my mind...' She turned the little bag over in her hand, fingering its intriguing lumpiness. 'Where did you get the hair to bind it?'

It was a few moments before he answered. 'The morning you left, you must have used my hairbrush,' he said quietly. 'There was a hair left in it— a strand of black silk. I'd kept it. I thought——' He stroked her hair with a kind of wonderment. 'I thought it might be all I had to remember you by.'

Sasha felt the tears start in her eyes. 'I came so close to losing you...'

He shook his head. 'You'll never lose me, Sasha. I'll always be here. And next time your gypsy soul needs to run, we'll run together.' His lips met hers and his hands slid down her body, pulling her close. 'I love you, little gypsy.'

Sasha felt the slumbering fires inside her waken and flare in response. 'I love you, Dirk.' And she knew that, at last, she had come home.

VOWS LaVyrle Spencer £2.99

When high-spirited Emily meets her father's new business rival,
Tom, sparks fly, and create a blend of pride and passion in this
compelling and memorable novel

LOTUS MOON Janice Kaiser £2.99

This novel vividly captures the futility of the Vietnam War and the
legacy it left. Haunting memories of the beautiful Lotus Moon fuel
Buck Michael's dangerous obsession, which only Amanda Parr can
help overcome.

SECOND TIME LUCKY Eleanor Woods £2.75

Danielle has been married twice. Now, as a young, beautiful widow,
can she back-track to the first husband whose life she left in ruins
with her eternal quest for entertainment and the high life?

**These three new titles will be out in bookshops from
September 1989.**

W🌐RLDWIDE

4 ROMANCES & 2 GIFTS - YOURS

ABSOLUTELY FREE!

An irresistible invitation from Mills & Boon! Please accept our offer of 4 free books, a pair of decorative glass oyster dishes and a special MYSTERY GIFT...Then, if you choose, go on to enjoy 6 more exciting Romances every month for just £1.35 each postage and packing free.

Send the coupon below at once to -
Reader Service, FREEPOST, P.O. Box 236, Croydon, Surrey CR9 9EL

✂ - *No stamp required* -

YES! Please rush me my **4 Free Romances and 2 FREE Gifts !** Please also reserve me a Reader Service Subscription. so I can look forward to receiving 6 Brand New Romances each month, for just £8.10 total. Post and packing is **free**, and there's a free monthly Mills & Boon Newsletter. If I choose not to subscribe I shall write to you within 10 days - I understand I can keep the books and gifts whatever I decide. I can cancel or suspend my subscription at any time, I am over18.

EP60R

NAME _____

ADDRESS _____

_____

_____ POSTCODE _____

SIGNATURE _____

The right is reserved to refuse an application and change the terms of this offer. You may be mailed with other offers as a result of this application. Offer expires Dec 31st 1989 and is limited to one per household. offer applies in the UK and Eire only. Overseas send for details